I0817962

NOT WELL

(A Camille Grace FBI Suspense Thriller—Book 3)

Kate Bold

Kate Bold

Bestselling author Kate Bold is author of the ALEXA CHASE SUSPENSE THRILLER series, comprising six books (and counting); the ASHLEY HOPE SUSPENSE THRILLER series, comprising six books (and counting); the CAMILLE GRACE FBI SUSPENSE THRILLER series, comprising five books (and counting); and the HARLEY COLE FBI SUSPENSE THRILLER series, comprising three books (and counting).

An avid reader and lifelong fan of the mystery and thriller genres, Kate loves to hear from you, so please feel free to visit www.kateboldauthor.com to learn more and stay in touch.

ISBN: 978-1-0943-9537-1

BOOKS BY KATE BOLD

ALEXA CHASE SUSPENSE THRILLER
THE KILLING GAME (Book #1)
THE KILLING TIDE (Book #2)
THE KILLING HOUR (Book #3)
THE KILLING POINT (Book #4)
THE KILLING FOG (Book #5)
THE KILLING PLACE (Book #6)

ASHLEY HOPE SUSPENSE THRILLER
LET ME GO (Book #1)
LET ME OUT (Book #2)
LET ME LIVE (Book #3)
LET ME BREATHE (Book #4)
LET ME FORGET (Book #5)
LET ME ESCAPE (Book #6)

CAMILLE GRACE FBI SUSPENSE THRILLER
NOT ME (Book #1)
NOT NOW (Book #2)
NOT WELL (Book #3)
NOT HER (Book #4)
NOT NORMAL (Book #5)

HARLEY COLE FBI SUSPENSE THRILLER
NOWHERE SAFE (Book #1)
NOWHERE LEFT (Book #2)
NOWHERE TO RUN (Book #3)

CHAPTER ONE

Brittany stumbled to the front of the boat with the sounds of jumbled zydeco music blaring behind her. She'd found it enjoyable as recently as three minutes ago but right now, it sounded like a hot mess. Who the hell built an entire style of music around the accordion, anyway?

She knew these weren't her true thoughts. No, she was simply irritated and maybe even a little alarmed because there was a searing pain currently tearing through her stomach. It had not been there until very recently. At first, she thought it was nothing but gas, maybe a little indigestion from the crawfish she'd had for dinner. But it quickly escalated into something much worse. This wasn't going to be just a visit to the bathroom with a terribly upset stomach; this was going to be a full-fledged purging of the stomach. And as this realization hit her, Brittany understood that she was going to have to make a very rough decision: rush down to the ladies' room on the lower level of the riverboat and hope a stall was available (and that she could make it that far) or run to the front of the boat, hope the crowd was thin, and hurl over the side.

The front being closer, that was the option she chose. And now, as the U-shaped rail of the riverboat came into view, she still didn't know if she was going to make it. And wouldn't that be something? Puking all over the bow of the *Wheeler's Delight* riverboat while the rest of the wedding party she was with continued to take shots and step a little closer to the men they'd been flirting with all afternoon.

But she did make it. And more than that, she was pleased to find that the front of the boat was indeed empty. The zydeco band, the happy hour prices at the bar at the back of the boat, and a buffet style dinner had drawn everyone away from the bow.

So when she reached the rail and perched slightly over it, there was no one there to see the terrible display. Still, it was embarrassing, especially when it came so hard and fast. She wasn't sure she'd ever retched so hard in her life. Fortunately, the sounds of the boat being propelled through the Mississippi River were just loud enough to cover up some of it.

Brittany threw up once, then twice, and then tried for a third time. Her stomach continued to insist there was more, that she needed to keep at it, but nothing else came up. She leaned over the rail. The beauty and majesty of the Mississippi spreading out behind her as she yakked into it. Exhausted, light-headed, and with her stomach cramping, Brittany stepped away from the rail. She wanted to instantly go find some water to rinse her mouth out but figured it would probably be a smart move to stay here just a while longer.

She was about to walk to the right, where a set of stairs led up to the second floor—the riverboat's first balcony level. But as she made her way over, she saw a boy sitting on one of the stairs. She wasn't sure how old he was—thirteen or fourteen, maybe. He was wearing a hooded sweatshirt and looking down at his hands. Probably because he'd just witnessed her little show.

"Huh," Brittany said. "Did you see all that?"

The boy said nothing, but he did look up at her. She didn't like the way he looked at her. His eyes looked menacing from under the hood and his hair hung in his face in a way that made him look older than he actually was.

Only…was that right? Maybe he *was* older and she had just seen him wrong at first.

She was about to say something like *There's no need to stare* when the boy got to his feet. And as he came walking quickly over to her, she saw that she *had* been wrong at first. He wasn't a boy. He was a fully grown man, just one of short stature. And by the time she pieced this together, he was on her, his hands coming forward. There was something in his hands and he was bringing them to her throat.

Brittany opened her mouth to scream but tasted a bit of bile in the back of her throat. Christ, was she going to puke again? Now, with this creep right in front of h—

Whatever it was he had in his hands came around her throat and with a set of small yet surprisingly strong hands, she was turned around quickly.

"Hey…" she said—or, rather, tried to say. Her stomach buckled and she did throw up again, but she was barely aware of it. Instead, all she could focus on was the feeling of being lifted and dropped. The world swayed, pivoted, and then fell.

After that, there was horrendous pain in her neck and head. She was pretty sure she hit the water at some point. It was cold, hard, but somehow also accepting.

Water started to fill her mouth, her nostrils, and her lungs and sometime after that, when her frantic brain finally realized she should maybe swim for the surface and cry for help, the life went flowing out of her, as if carried away by the flow of the Mississippi River.

CHAPTER TWO

Camille already liked her New Orleans apartment much more than the place she'd had in Birmingham, but there were times when she felt that it was haunted by the ghost of her sister. Even though she now had reason to believe Nanette was still alive, her sister's presence seemed to loom over the place. It had been especially bad ever since she'd found out that her family had been keeping secrets from her. As Camille dug deeper into her sister's cold case, the sensation grew ever worse, like a strange humidity within the apartment.

But she loved the apartment itself and all it stood for. At first, she thought it was just the freedom of living on her own again, but after a week or so, she came to understand that it was the apartment itself. The neighborhood was really nothing special; she was about eight blocks away from the bustling energy of where the French Quarter began and just far enough away from any other touristy places to keep the streets quiet and reserved.

It was a small place, so she'd gotten a good deal on it. There was an exposed beam that ran up through the floor and connected to the ceiling, serving as the separating article between her small living room and even smaller kitchen. The hardwood floors were old but in a special sort of charming way, and the window by her small kitchen table looked out onto a small strip of puny forest between the complex's back lot and a small park.

In other words, not too shabby for a second shot—for a shot at starting over.

She'd also purchased a small couch from a second-hand furniture store in town. It was the only piece of furniture in her living room, but she loved it. It's where she read and relaxed, where she napped and occasionally watched television. But, more than anything else, it's where she sat when she went over the details of her sister's case.

She'd only managed to find a few notes on the disappearance of one Nanette Grace from nearly fifteen years ago. A young woman that seemed to have simply disappeared without a trace one night after performing with a small up-and-coming jazz band in the French Quarter. Most had presumed her dead, but she now had reason to believe her sister was very much alive. She printed them out in secret from her secluded little office at the field office but had elected to take them to her apartment and leave them there. She'd not yet fully earned the trust of her new assistant director, a friendly yet no-nonsense woman named Marie McCutcheon, and the last thing she wanted was for McCutcheon to find that she was looking around in case files from over a decade ago. Not to mention case files pertaining to a personal matter.

Currently, though, it was not the files on Nanette's disappearance that interested her. Instead, she was looking through her Aunt Deanna's social media. Not that Deanna was *really* her aunt; that's just how Camille had always thought of her. Although, as of about ten days ago, she was finding it quite hard to think anything positive about Deanna Lewiston. As a constant fixture in Camille's life since birth, Deanna had always been fun and dependable, helpful and nurturing.

But ten days ago, her father had let it slip that Deanna had seen Nanette twelve years ago—three years *after* Nanette had disappeared. And all this time, no one had told her. She'd been left in the dark for reasons she didn't care to think about. This sort of betrayal from her father didn't really surprise her, but when it came from Deanna, it was heartbreaking.

Deanna had texted twice in the past ten days. She had no idea that Camille knew about the visit She'd just been checking in, wanting to see when they could get together again. Camille had ignored both texts, not quite ready to face her just yet.

For the past two afternoons, Camille had been going through Deanna's social media accounts. The woman was a bit of a homebody and, though she had Facebook, Twitter, and Instagram accounts, she wasn't very active on any of them. In fact, her last Twitter post had come nearly two full years ago, providing a link to a local pottery class. Still, despite Deanna's inactivity, her accounts provided a snapshot into the people she knew. And while Camille had no illusions of accidentally stumbling across a Facebook page for Nanette, she thought there might be clues of some kind. It was a very faint trail of breadcrumbs to follow, but it at least gave her the smallest bit of hope. Besides…one of the main reasons she took the bureau job in New Orleans was to be closer to the community where she'd been raised. And she'd known it would eventually lead to her looking deeper into her sister's disappearance.

Camille had been looking through the accounts of Deanna's social media friends for nearly three hours when she came across a face that looked eerily familiar. It was a woman named Rose Dawson, from Oxford, North Carolina. With just a passing glance, the woman bore a striking resemblance to Nanette. The age was right, and the hair color was spot on.

Camille's chest tightened for only a moment, though. A glance of more than two seconds revealed that it was not Nanette. The angle of the eyes wasn't right, and the lips were too full. Even though she'd not seen her sister in fifteen years, she could tell this woman was not her. While she knew Nanette would not be the eighteen-year-old version of the girl Camille remembered, she had no doubt that something inside of her—be it her instincts or the very core of her heart—would recognize her sister.

So she scrolled past Rose Dawson and continued to search. Within a few more profiles, her phone buzzed in her hand. She was fully expecting it to be Deanna again. She knew it would *not* be her father because he'd been avoiding her. Not only had he angered her, but he was also afraid she was going to continue to push him to get treatment for the cancer diagnosis he'd been dealt nearly a year ago.

But when she reached her finger up to cancel the notification, she saw a name she'd thought of a few times in the past ten days. Zack Hayes. A zoologist out of Chalmette, Zack taught at a community college up that way and helped the smaller police departments from time to time when it came to coyote and gator attacks. They'd spoken only briefly during her time on her last case but it had stuck with her—and him, too, given that he'd tried convincing her to stick around and have dinner with him. She'd ultimately declined, because she wasn't ready to date having just moved to a new city, and she'd been waiting for his text ever since.

Didn't want to be presumptuous and call first, the text read. **So I figured I'd text. Now that I've officially texted, can I call?**

She smiled, glad to be looking away from the monotonous stream of Facebook profiles. And rather than respond to the text, she called him instead. It rang only a single time before he answered.

"Is this like a powerplay or something?" he asked. "You had to call me to make the first move?"

"This isn't a move," she argued. "Sorry if you feel emasculated."

"Not at all. If anything, it feels nice not to be the one to make the first call. So…how are you? How are things in N'ollins?"

"I'm still getting acclimated. And by the way, no one in this city *actually* talks like that. Well…maybe a few. But no one says the city name like that."

"I'll make a note of that. It'll be good to know for the trip I'm about to take out to your neck of the woods."

She smiled, instantly excited about the news. "And what brings you my way?"

"My great aunt's memorial service."

"Oh…oh, I'm sorry."

"Eh, at the risk of sounding insensitive, I barely knew her. I'm really just going to support my mother. They were really close. But yeah…I'll be there in two days. The thing is…I won't really have a lot of time to spend. I have to get back home pretty quickly. So that really only leaves me with a very unorthodox suggestion."

"Which is?"

"There's a potluck afterwards, at the church my mother attends. Want to meet me there?"

It wasn't at all what she was expecting. Everything her told her to say no; even though she was very interested in Zack, the situation was just too weird. Even stranger, though, was that when she opened her mouth to answer, "Sounds good," came out.

"Really? That's not too weird for you?"

"Oh, it's all kinds of weird," Camille said. "But it'll be interesting. I guess that's the right word to use. What's the church?"

"Cornerstone Baptist on Weaving Street. You know it?"

Camille was glad they weren't speaking face to face because she couldn't help but cringe. Yes, she knew the church. It had some very unpleasant family connections for her—connections she'd rather not bring to the surface.

"I know it," she said. "And now that I think of it, I don't know—"

Her phone beeped in her ear as another call came through. She quickly glanced at the call display and saw that it was the office. More notably, it was Assistant Director McCutcheon.

"Hey, Zack, I have another call and I have to take it. It's my director."

"Say no more. Want me to just give you a buzz when I get into town?"

"Sure thing. Do that. And thanks for reaching out."

"Hey, you're the one that called *me*," he pointed out, and then ended the call.

Camille switched over to the other line. As it was nearing 10:30 at night, she could only assume the call from McCutcheon would put her on a case—if not immediately tonight, then tomorrow.

"This is Agent Grace," she answered.

"Grace, I need you to be in my office at 7:30 tomorrow morning. There's a case I'd like you to run with."

"I can do that. Any preliminary notes or material I can look over in the meantime?"

"We're still getting it all together. Some details are still coming in from the State Police. I should have it all in the morning."

"Understood."

"I haven't decided if I'm going to pair you with someone yet," McCutcheon said. "If I *do* make that decision, are you good working with Palmer? He had very nice things to say about you and the two of you seem to work well together."

"Yes, Palmer would be fine. I have no objections to that."

"Good. Then I'll see you in the morning."

They ended the call with Camille feeling a little off-center. McCutcheon was very easy-going and conversational. The two supervisors she'd had in the past had been more like drill sergeants than supervisors. And though she still didn't quite have her new assistant director figured out, she did feel more at ease in her new location than she'd expected. McCutcheon was one of the reasons, Palmer was another, and her growing love for the city—a city she'd always viewed with a bit of resentment from her childhood years—was another reason.

Putting the phone down, Camille also started to gather up the few files she had on Nanette. She'd done enough for tonight, especially considering that she was already fairly certain she'd never make any progress on the case. Too much time had elapsed; even if she managed to find a thread somewhere in the old files, it would be old and buried by now.

Camille readied herself for bed and found that when she was under the covers, she simply wasn't ready for sleep. She was thinking of Nanette, sure, but also of Cornerstone Baptist Church. It was not a church she'd ever attended, but one that her mother had often spoken of. And what really hurt was that she would probably end up canceling on Zack just to avoid the memories of her mother and of Nanette whom, on more than on occasion, had sung in the choir at Cornerstone Baptist on special revival Sundays.

Under her covers, Camille could feel her past and present starting to collide. It was heavy on her heart and made her wonder if, despite her recent rekindled love for New Orleans, her past would end up pushing her away from it all.

CHAPTER THREE

As Camille stepped onto the elevator, she heard quickened footsteps behind her. As she stepped in and turned around to press the 2 on the wall panel, she saw Scott Palmer hurrying towards her.

"Hold the doors, would you, Grace?"

Camille grinned at him as she placed her hand against the side of the door. Palmer hurried forward and joined her in the elevator. It was quite clear from his tousled hair and heavy breathing that he'd been running late this morning and doing everything he could to make it in to work on time. Somehow, though, he still had the sun-tinged skin and messy-hair that looked cute—the kind of man that could literally roll out of bed and come to work still looking like a treat.

"I take it McCutcheon called you about the new case?" Camille asked.

"She did. Around eleven or so last night. Did she give you any details?"

"None. I'm just as in the dark as you are."

"Great," he said, doing his best to straighten out his hair by looking in the murky, steel reflection of the control panel. "This should be a fun meeting, then."

"Can't be too urgent if she allowed it to wait until this morning," Camille pointed out.

"True." He was finished with his hair by the time the elevator came to a stop, dinging and sliding the doors open. Camille stepped out first and Palmer followed closely behind. "You think we walk in together like this, or is it a bit cheesy?"

"Depends," Camille said. "How does McCutcheon feel about punctuality?"

"Good point."

Palmer sped up, blasting ahead of Camille and turning left into McCutcheon's office ahead of her. Camille hurried a bit but not to the comical lengths Palmer had shown. When she entered the office, Palmer was already taking a seat in one of the two chairs in front of McCutcheon's desk.

"Good morning, Ms. Assistant Director," Palmer said with a smile.

“Same to you,” McCutcheon said. She then nodded with a smile to Camille as she entered the office. McCutcheon was reading something on her laptop and scribbling information down on a legal pad to her left. “I should have the two of you out of here fairly quickly. I’ve got everything we need to get started on this; the details are a little strange yet very specific.”

“What is it, exactly?” Camille asked as she took the other chair.

“So far, we’ve got two victims. No ID on the first one yet. All we know for sure is that it’s a male, he was found in the Mississippi River, and there is suspected strangulation involved. But the most recent one was found last night around nine o’clock and has been identified as twenty-three year-old Brittany Gable. She was out on a riverboat with a bachelorette party last night. She was also found in the river, with signs of strangulation around her neck.”

“How far apart were the bodies found?” Camille asked.

“We’re looking at a difference of two days. In terms of geographical space, the bodies were found exactly ninety-one miles apart from one another. Brittany Gable was found floating in the water just twenty miles outside of the city.”

“Have any statements been taken from the other women at the bachelorette party?”

“Yes, and I’m including all of that in the case package I’m about to send you. And frankly, until we get this first victim properly identified, the bachelorette party may be your only viable avenue.”

“Have our guys already got access to the first body?” Palmer asked.

“The State PD is transporting it as we speak.” McCutcheon drummed her fingers on the edge of her desk and looked nervously at both of them. “Two bodies in the river, one of which we *know* came off of a riverboat. Being that we’re rapidly coming up on the peak time for tourist season, I can’t stress enough how important it is that this case be closed as soon as possible. I would have called you in last night, but we’re just getting all of the details necessary to really get started…to have any links at all. The public gets scared and it reflects on the tourists. And if the word about this gets out before we’ve wrapped it, it’s going to also start affecting tourists. When *that* happens, we get pressure from people like governors and committees, and I’d love to avoid that. I know it sounds very backwards and uncaring, but it’s the sad truth of the matter. If tourist season is hit in any way, local businesses are going to suffer. And I don’t need to tell you who state representatives are going to be looking at, right?”

“So then we should start right away,” Camille said.

“Check with my assistant for print copies of the files. The emails were sent the moment you stepped into the office. But really, I think you can save a lot of time by heading to the Fourth District police station. Two of the girls from the bachelorette party are scheduled to be there at nine o’ clock. And given the sensitive nature of this case, I feel pretty certain the police captain will gladly let you run it.”

“Anything else?” Palmer asked.

“No. If this turns out to be a longer case, I *would* like you reporting back to me every twelve hours or so. I’d like to have *something* to tell the governor or his minions if they do decide to call and breathe down the bureau’s neck.”

Needing no further guidance, Camille and Palmer excused themselves. In total, they’d spent less than five minutes in the office. It was unlike most of Camille’s experiences back in Alabama. Her supervisor there had been a bear of a man that felt that every bit of information needed to be drilled into the heads of his agents before he sent them out. The same meeting she’d just had with McCutcheon may have taken half an hour.

“Question,” Palmer asked when they got back into the elevator. “What kind of bachelorette party takes place on a riverboat?”

“There’s booze on riverboats,” Camille said. “What do you have against riverboats?”

“Nothing. Just seems a little lame to me.”

“Well, it was early in the night. Maybe it was just one stage of a much larger night out.”

They were both opening their emails, scanning through the PDF of the case files they’d been sent. There were transcripts of the interviews the police had conducted with some of the women at the bachelor party as well as a few others that had been on the boat. But even a quick glance told Camille that very little of it would help.

“You want to get the print-outs from the assistant?” Palmer asked. “I’ll get a car and meet you out front.”

Camille nodded and they split up at as they stepped out of the elevator. Camille continued to scan the documents as she walked, scrolling through the bit of information they’d been given. Potential strangulation, both found in the river, and the victims were different genders. At face value, the murders spoke of intent and purpose. Unless it was a very strong coincidence, the similarities suggested these weren’t random murders—that the killer had some sort of purpose or reason in mind.

This was both good *and* bad. Good because if they found the reason, it made the killer a bit easier to find. And bad because if they *couldn't* discover the reason, they were already a very big step behind.

CHAPTER FOUR

McCutcheon was right; the police captain and the two officers that had been ready to question the young women from the bachelorette party seemed eager to hand the case off. Camille supposed it was because they had the same fears as McCutcheon. No one wanted state officials or individuals from the government poking and prodding into a case they were assigned to. Being able to hand it off to another organization was like washing your hands of the matter, shucking the responsibility.

There were two of them already waiting when Camille and Palmer arrived at the downtown station. They'd been led into a conference room in the back of the building. They both had to-go coffees and a plate of pastries had been placed in the center of the table. The woman sitting on the right side of the table was very petite and looked exhausted. The immediate area around her eyes was red and puffy, indicating she'd been crying a lot recently. The other woman was an almost stereotypical bombshell. Slightly tall, blonde, flawless complexion, and a body that you could tell was perfect even though she was wearing nothing to really show it off. She also looked rather tired but her beauty hid most of it.

"Ladies, I'm agent Camille Grace, with the FBI. This is my partner, Agent Palmer. We want to ask some questions about the events of yesterday afternoon, leading up to Brittany's death. I understand you've likely already been questioned but I assure you, this is necessary. Can I start with getting your names and how you knew Brittany?"

The blonde spoke first, in a tired but sweet voice. "I'm Lexi Dean. I was Brittany's college roommate for freshman and sophomore year."

"I'm Rose Keever," the waifish, red-eyed girl said. "I've been friends with Brittany since middle school. Even when she went to college and I slummed it out in menial jobs back home, we were always in touch."

"And you were both with the bachelorette party?" Camille asked. "How do you both know the bride-to-be?"

"We all grew up in the same town," Lexi said. "Dunnbrook, about an hour west of Baton Rouge. I did sort of drift apart from my friend group when I went to college but summer vacations brought me right back into the fold."

"So let's talk about the bachelorette party," Palmer said. "What did you ladies do before boarding the riverboat yesterday afternoon?"

"We started with lunch first," Rose said. "We had lunch at this little greasy spoon diner that Brittany always liked. We left there and went to find some early happy hour deals."

"So you started drinking early?" Camille said.

"Yes, that's correct," Lexi said. "Nothing overboard, though. We all had martinis and then a shot of tequila. And then we went out and got on the riverboat."

"And during all of this, did Brittany seem fine?" Camille asked.

"She did," Lexi said. "I mean, she was *peak* Brittany. Making jokes. Flirting with the bartender. She wasn't really ever the life of the party, but it wasn't much of a party if she wasn't around, you know?"

"When you got on the riverboat, would you say Brittany or anyone else in the group was inebriated?"

"I don't think so," Lexi said. "I wasn't, and I doubt Brittany was."

"Same here," Rose said.

"At any point before you learned that Brittany had gone missing, would you say you had gotten to that point?"

"I was definitely buzzed," Lexi said. "But still, when we figured out that Brittany had gone missing, I sobered up pretty quickly."

"How long do you think it took you to realize she was gone?" Palmer asked.

"No more than half an hour," Rose answered.

"Yeah, she told us her stomach was hurting. She said it came out of nowhere. We figured it might have just been something she'd eaten. There was this big buffet on the boat and I think we all went a little nuts on the shrimp and crawfish."

"Yeah," Rose agreed. "When she said she had to go find a restroom, I figured she'd just eaten too much, or maybe got a bad shrimp or two."

"The cops said there was puke in the water and on the front of the boat from where they think she threw up overboard," Lexi said. "I hate that's how she spent her last few moments."

"Ladies, when you were on the boat, how many of you were there?" Palmer asked.

"Five, including Regina, the bride-to-be," Lexi said.

"And out of your group, did any of you get a little over-friendly with anyone else?" Palmer asked.

"What do you mean?" Rose asked.

Side-stepping pleasantries, Camille said, "Were any of you flirting with any men on board?"

"No," Lexi said. "I mean, there was this older gentleman that I danced with for a minute or two. But I was just being funny, trying to brighten his day up, you know? He and his wife were celebrating their fortieth wedding anniversary. But I'd hardly call that flirting."

"Were there any men that tried hitting on any of you?" Camille asked.

"Not in any obvious way," Rose said. "Not that I could see, anyway. I mean, we were a group of loud women with a bachelorette party. We did get *some* men looking our way, but it was too early in the day, I guess."

"What about any sort of altercations?" Palmer asked. "Was there ever anything that caused strife or unpleasantness. Even something as minor as accidentally bumping into someone as you made your way around the boat?"

Both women thought about this for a moment. Rose began to slowly shake her head. "Not that I can recall—not for me, anyway. Of course, I can't speak for Brittany."

She seemed to clinch up as she said her deceased friend's name. Her bottom lip started to tremble and she slowly looked down at her hands, resting on top of the table.

"Same for me," Lexi said. "I had no problems, but I don't know about Brittany. If she did have any issue like that, she never mentioned it to me."

Camille was starting to sense that this line of questioning was coming to an end. On the surface, she could not detect any sense of dishonesty from the women. She'd seen loss and grief in people before and what she saw in Rose seemed legitimate.

"I wonder if the two of you took any pictures or videos during the course of the day."

"I did," Rose said, wiping a tear away.

"Yeah, me, too," Lexi said. "And I'm pretty sure Regina did, as well."

"I'm going to ask that you both send me any pictures or videos," Camille said. "I'll leave my email address with the officer that's been in charge here. I'd appreciate it if you could have Regina and the other girls do the same. Can you do that for me as soon as possible?"

"Absolutely," Lexi said, already taking out her phone.

Rose looked to Camille, directly at her, locking eyes. "Do you think you'll figure it out? Do you think you'll be able to find who did this?"

"I certainly hope so. I think it's early enough where we're likely to have some success."

She was careful not to say anything more, not wanting to promise results that she would not be able to deliver.

"One last thing," Camille said. "Can either of you think of any people that may have held a grudge against Brittany? Anyone at all?"

"No," Lexi said. "And I know it seems like a quick, easy answer. but I spent a lot of time last night and this morning trying to figure that out for myself. Like…who would want to do this to Brittany? She never…I mean, she never had a bad thing to say about anyone. I don't know that anyone on this planet would have anything against her. Brittany was…well, she was sort of the best."

Rose nodded in agreement, again fighting with her emotions. Camille looked to Palmer and he nodded to her, letting her know that as far as he was concerned, they were done here. And while Camille agreed, she also hated to leave without answers.

However, maybe their next stop would be more lucrative. If Brittany's friends couldn't give them any answers, maybe Brittany's body would offer up some clues.

CHAPTER FIVE

When they arrived at the coroner's office, Camille couldn't help but feel as if the timing of it all might be some sort of good omen. As soon as they were led back to the room where Brittany Gable's body was being stored, the coroner had been called to the back of the building to receive another body. This turned out to be the body of the first victim, the as-of-now nameless male that had been shipped to the bureau's coroner of choice.

Once the paperwork was filled out and proper guidelines were adhered to, Camille and Palmer found themselves standing in a large examination room with both victims and the coroner. The coroner, a middle-aged man with graying hair and intense, staring eyes, looked to the newly arrived corpse with both irritation and disgust. While he observed the body, Camille did her own quick look over the bodies—starting with the fresher and perhaps more relevant body of Brittany Gable.

"You received Ms. Gabel's body right away, correct?" Palmer asked as Camille looked the body over.

"That's right. It was really just because I was closer, I believe." He sneered, looking at the body of the first victim. "Might be a little difficult to find any real connection at this point. Looks like this fellow was in the water for quite a while."

While the coroner got a closer look at the first victim, Camille continued to study Brittany. The signs of possible strangulation were clear; there was a visible bruise around her neck, right across the windpipe. There was also a good deal of scratching and abrasions of the skin between the bruise and the underside of her chin. Camille supposed that whatever the killer had choked her with must have slipped. She figured it was also a sage assumption that perhaps the slippage may have been what resulted in Brittany falling into the river.

Other than the mark on her neck, there were no obvious signs of an attack. She did wonder, though, what the coroner may find in her stomach. How much shrimp and crawfish *had* she eaten? And that produced another thought to ponder: had the killer seen her in a state of illness and followed her around the boat hoping to somehow take advantage?

Done with Brittany, she moved over to the first victim. His skin was water-logged and pruny. He was also very white. Camille guessed him to be in his early-to-mid fifties. His had a pudgy face with no real fat accumulation around his stomach. His hair had once been brown but had been in the process of quickly going gray when he'd died.

Having looked over both bodies, she took a moment to remind herself that they were people that had lost their lives—not just a case to be solved. She sometimes found that when she was faced with more than one body at a time, she almost subconsciously tried to treat it as a puzzle and not an effort to find justice for the recently deceased.

"You may want this," the coroner said, hanging a large evidence bag over to her. Inside were the man's clothes. They looked to have been somewhat dried but when she unclasped the top of the bag, the rank smell that came out told her that they'd only been air-dried....which was good if they intended to get any sort of evidence off of them.

"Do you have anything off of Ms. Gable?" Palmer asked.

"Right over there," the coroner said, pointing to the counter along the back wall. Camille looked over in that direction and saw a set of clothes spread out on metal trays. A smaller one contained a set of earrings, a necklace, an expensive-looking ring, and an Apple watch.

So it wasn't a robbery of any sort, Camille noted. And based on the fact that Brittany had been fully clothed and apparently attacked on a riverboat, she doubted the attack had been of a sexual nature, either. That meant the killer was doing it just for the act of murder—which often made for a much more dangerous suspect.

Camille looked at the bag in her hands, wondering if there might be some answers hiding in the mildew-rich stink. "Where can I find gloves and a tray or two of my own?"

"Gloves are the first drawer on the right, the trays are all up in the overhead cabinets. Make yourself at home."

Camille went through the mentioned drawers and cabinets, slapping on a pair of latex gloves and taking down a large, metal tray. She dumped out the man's clothes—a pair of khaki shorts that looked to be of the golfing variety, and a Polo shirt. The shirt had no pockets so she dismissed it right away. If there had been any DNA evidence on it, it had been washed away in the river.

"You know," Palmer said, stepping up beside her, "the original reports said the police didn't find a wallet on him. You know…if that's what you're looking for."

"Yes, I know. I'm seeing if there's anything else."

"Seven dollars in cash and a single sour candy were found in his pockets," the coroner called. "A cheap wristwatch was taken from his body but that was all. Those items are in another bag if you'd like to see them."

"Maybe in a bit," Camille said.

She had a hunch that she wasn't even fully aware she'd come to until she had poured the clothes out onto the trays. Since there was no connection between the victims in age or gender, the only thing that really linked them, other than strangulation, was that their bodies had been disposed of in the Mississippi River. It made her wonder if the river may link them in yet another way. If Brittany Gable had been strangled and then tossed from a riverboat, she supposed there was a chance the same was true of the male victim. It was a bit of a stretch but certainly worth the digging to either confirm the theory or eliminate it.

She checked inside the back pockets, finding nothing but wet lint and silt from the riverbank. She then checked the front pockets and found the same. Just to be certain, she grabbed the lining of each pocket and pulled them inside out. Almost right away, she saw something that had gone overlooked by the initial investigators. There was a folded piece of paper stuck to the lining of the left pocket.

She plucked it off and slowly unfolded it. As she did, it became clear that it wasn't just a scrap of paper, but a piece of sturdier material. At first, she thought it might be a movie ticket but when she had it fully unfolded, she saw it for what it was.

"I'll be damned," Palmer said from beside her.

They were looking at a soggy ticket for passage on a riverboat.

The ink was smeared and partially washed away but the majority of the date and the name of the boat remained. The boat was named The *Whistlin' Pig* and the ticket had been purchased three days ago.

"*Whistlin' Pig*," Camille said. "That's not the name of the one Brittany was on, was it?"

"Don't think so," Palmer said, grabbing his phone to scroll through the digital files they'd been provided. It took him only a few seconds to find it and when he did, he started shaking his head. "Nope. Brittany and the bachelorette party were on *Wheeler's Delight*." And then, under his breath, he added; "Jesus, who names these things?"

With the ticket still held in her gloved hands, Camille walked over to the coroner, already measuring the body of the first victim. "This ticket says this gentleman was on board a riverboat three days ago. Not sure of the time, but let's just pinpoint noon as a safe base. Would you say his condition lines him up with that timeframe?"

"It's very likely," the coroner said. "Though, of course, him being in the water for so long is going to make any sort of guesses pretty flimsy. I'd have to get inside to get an accurate picture of it all."

Camille nodded as she peered under the man's chin, looking for any signs of strangulation that had been listed in the report. She could see it easily, but it had started to fade considerably. His was more pronounced than the marks on Brittany's neck. It seemed the killer had done a more accurate job on the first victim.

She stepped away, thinking. She returned the ticket to the trays with the man's clothes, snapping a picture of it with her phone.

"You know," Palmer said, "it's early enough where I think we can probably get to those boats before they start the day's expeditions. I have no idea if riverboats have security cameras on board or not, but I think it's worth looking into."

"I think you're right," Camille said. "And even if not, I think it might do us some good to visit the final places both of our victims saw." She looked back to the two dead bodies on the tables and added: "And the places the killer chose to strike."

CHAPTER SIX

"Hey, look at the dwarf!"

"Do you think you can get my letter to Santa, elf?"

"Say hi to the ants for me!"

He'd heard them all, plus thousands more that just weren't quite as memorable. And as he coasted along on the Mississippi River on a small commuter boat, he could hear some of them as clear as day. Several people milled about, mostly locals but a few tourists mingling in. These were older people with no jobs to rush off to, or maybe the few younger folks he saw were just enjoying s quiet morning on the river.

He looked to hide in the midst of normalcy. It helped him to cope, helped him to figure out what was wrong with him.

Even as early as the sixth grade, it had become apparent that he was going to be almost absurdly small. He'd been relentlessly picked on about it and had taken a few beatings because of his small stature in high school. Because of the trauma in high school—including being stuffed into a gym locker and abandoned for three hours with electrical tape over his mouth—he'd not bothered to even think of college.

The years between high school and now had been a bit better, though not perfect. Grown-ups sometimes were assholes, too, after all. And really, as long as he wore clothes that covered most of his frame and a hat or hoody that hid his face, most people that randomly passed him on the street thought he was a kid. A teenager, maybe, moody and always looking down at his feet with his face hidden.

And when he *did* get those sorts of comments thrown his way, he didn't really even care anymore. He was twenty-nine now, and had learned how to use his short stature to his advantage. Being of such a small size allowed him to go about most of his day unseen and unnoticed. And given what he'd been up to as of late, it made things *much* easier.

He had started to understand, though, that the constant taunting and teasing as a kid had planted something inside of him. He recognized the extreme anger in his heart; he *knew* it was there. But he didn't see the need to change it. The anger and hatred he felt was a part of him now—

as much a part of him as his small size. And rather than let it simmer inside of him and fester into something even worse, he was choosing to let it out in a way that he felt was not only natural, but also beneficial.

He was using it to cleanse the world of people that had no regard for nature. And he was starting in the area of the state where he'd been born, raised, and teased relentlessly. He loved the city, the river, the smell and sights of the street and trees alike. And day by day, it was getting worse and worse. His sanctuary was being taken away from him.

He'd noticed the need for it a few months ago. He'd started to realize how people had no real respect for the city, for the outlying areas that grew so green and great. Perhaps worst of all, it was mostly locals. Tourists to New Orleans and the surrounding area were often fascinated by the scenery and did their best to maintain some degree of respect. This naturally changed when the party-crowd was involved, people that were just interested in getting wasted down on Bourbon Street.

But the locals were naturally easier to study and track. Like, for instance, the woman he was currently watching. She was sitting on the other side of the boat's back end on the pond he'd been stationed beside all morning. She looked to be nearing forty and was rather pretty. She'd had a few conversations on her cellphone and even as he watched her, she was brainlessly tearing up a donut and tossing it out into the water. When the boat had cleared enough space, some of the braver ducks would come in from off the banks and gobble up the chunks.

Of course, it was nothing new to see people feeding ducks bread. Everyone did it even though it was discouraged by some of the signs scattered around parks throughout the city. He knew that bread offered no nutritional value to ducks and it often caused malnutrition in ducklings. Worse than that, this woman was feeding them *donuts* which were loaded with sugars that were deadly not only to ducks but to the fish that would almost certainly grab the pieces left behind and it would kill them as well.

To some, he knew this act would go totally unseen. The woman was attractive and really, what harm was she causing?

But it made him furious—almost irrationally so. He supposed it didn't help that his attention was also drawn to the railing behind her. He saw a dried wad of chewing gum that someone had stuck on the underside. He was quite sure the woman hadn't done this (it looked too hardened and old), but it only fueled his anger.

He watched the woman absently toss the last of her donut into the water. She then made another phone call, spoke for about forty seconds, and then ended it. She looked upset, not quite sad but clearly bothered. He figured it likely had something to do with the phone calls. But her emotional state did not sway him one way or the other.

When she got to her feet a few minutes later, he'd already made his decision. There was another ten minutes or so remaining in the ride. They'd be docking near Woldenberg Park. It was a route he knew well, as he rode it at least once a week—and had been for the past four years or so, with the exception of the winter months.

He also knew the boat well. Which meant as he, too, got up, he was able to follow after the woman without seeming too obvious. As he walked to the other side of the boat to fall in behind her, he glanced out and watched three ducks fighting over the final few bits of the donut. But even further out, over near the thin marshes alongside the river where there were no banks, he spotted two fishermen. They were tearing through the reeds and weeds, not caring how they made the scenery look, not giving a damn about the litter they'd likely leave behind.

He clenched his fists and took a very deep breath. And by the time the woman was once again in his sights, he was focused. Focused on her and on his anger.

And, as he placed his right hand into his pocket, he was also focused on the thick strand of bailing wire, already curled from the last two necks he's wrapped it around. He gripped it tightly and followed behind the woman, gaining on her with every single step.

CHAPTER SEVEN

The *Whistlin' Pig* was still docked at the wooden pier when Camille and Palmer arrived at 10:25. According to the schedule, its first trip out was at 10:55, and the little ticket kiosk just off the pier hadn't even yet started selling tickets for it. Camille flashed her badge to the man at the still-closed kiosk and he allowed them access by lowering a thin chain between the sidewalk and the pier.

When they came to the boat, there was no way on board; the little connector walkway that extended out onto the dock had not been unlatched from the boat's interior. There were three men on the back of the boat, watching Camille and Palmer as they approached. One of them looked very confused, casting a look back to the ticket kiosk to see how these two folks had gotten by.

"We're with the FBI,' Palmer said, clarifying things for them. He showed his badge as he said: "I'm Agent Palmer, and this is my partner, Agent Grace. Would you mind if we came aboard?"

Two of the men shared a puzzled look while the third, an older man that had lost most of his hair and wore a tweed coat, stared at Camille and Palmer in disbelief. One of the men nodded and stepped forward. He unlatched the little metal walkway and lowered it to the dock.

"Mind if I ask what you need to see the boat for?" he asked.

"You the driver?" Palmer asked.

"I am. Driver…captain, whatever you prefer."

The second man, still standing in his original spot by the balding man, spoke up, too. "And I'm the owner. I own this one and five others."

"Oh, that's perfect," Camille said. "We're investigating two murders and both of them seem to have occurred on riverboats that originate from this area."

"What?" the driver said. "Murders?"

"Yes, sir," Camille said.

"On *this* boat?" The owner asked. "On the *Whistlin' Pig*?"

"That's right. We don't have a name for the gentleman just yet but we did find a ticket in his pocket, putting him on this boat right around the time he was killed. His body was discovered in the river."

"What was the other boat?" the owner asked. He looked like he was about to be sick. Camille could see his eyes widen and then narrow over and over again; it was the look of a man that was trying very hard to process some very unfortunate news.

"*Wheeler's Delight*," Palmer answered.

"That's not mine," the owner said as a wave of relief came over his face.

"And what's your name by the way?" Palmer asked.

"Christopher Jefferson." Jefferson extended his hand to be shook, but in a way that meant nothing; it was clear he did this same thing at least ten to twenty times a day, greeting people properly.

"Mr. Jefferson, would you happen to know who *does* own *Wheeler's Delight*?"

"Not personally. But the company is called River Runners. They tend to run higher-end boats. The sort used for parties, miniature cruises, and things like that. My fleet is typically for casual sightseers."

"About how many people per ride?" Palmer asked.

"On a slow day, maybe forty. But on weekends or peak tourist season, I can fill my boats to max capacity, which is one ninety."

"So three days ago…what were the numbers like?" Camille asked.

"That was a Sunday. So…probably around one hundred, I suppose. I can check my logs if you need a specific number."

"I don't know if that's necessary. We're looking for a very specific male that we have yet to ID."

"You're welcome to check the camera footage."

"There are security cameras on deck?" Palmer asked.

"Two, in fact. One is mobile. We use it only when we suspect there's going to be a problem between passengers. Maybe a drunken brawl, you know? It happens a bit too much, in my opinion. But yes, we also have a stationary one located right there."

He pointed to Camille's right, to a small box that was so perfectly embedded into the corner of the deck that it looked as if it had been built in. A small rectangular shape with rounded edges broke the decoy apart, though.

"That would be great. How soon can you get it to us?" Camille asked.

Jefferson seemed very pleased as he took out his cellphone. "Hang tight and I can have it for you in about five minutes or so." He chuckled and said, "I swear, everything is run by an app these days, isn't it?"

While Jefferson opened up the app for his security camera, Camille thought it might be a good idea to have a walk around the boat. While it was a riverboat by definition, complete with a paddlewheel on the back, the *Whistlin' Pig* was much smaller than most other riverboats that trotted up and down the Mississippi; and Camille hoped that would play in their favor.

From the helm, she and Palmer walked along the entire first of two floors. Inside, there was a small game room and a quaint sitting area. At the back of the seating area was a small bar. She walked the narrow stairway to the second floor and found nothing more than a lot of open-floor seating. It was decorated and set up quite nicely but truly was a much smaller experience than most other riverboats offered. As she walked back through to join Jefferson and the other two men, she saw a young man at the bar. He was setting things up for the day, a reminder to Camille that the *Whistlin' Pig* would be taking off soon.

When they rejoined Jefferson at the back of the boat, he was chatting with the captain. The balding man had stepped down off the boat and was chatting with the person at the ticket kiosk.

"I think I've got what you need," Jefferson said, showing them his phone. "We only run one trip for the *Whistlin' Pig* on Sundays, and that shoves off at three in the afternoon. So right here, this is footage as everyone is loading up. It's not the best angle, but you should be able to clearly see everyone that steps on board."

"Do you mind?" Camille asked, opening her hand to take his phone.

"Not at all."

He handed it over gladly, leaving Camille and Palmer to lean against the back rail and go through the footage. The controls were very easy and she had a handle on it within seconds. As she scrolled to speed things up, she heard Palmer quietly counting to himself as each new person on the video footage stepped on board. There were several seconds and, at one point, even several minutes between passengers as they stepped on board.

When Palmer counted out *"Thirty-one,"* she paused the footage.

The man that crossed in front of the camera was the dead man they'd seen on a slab in the coroner's office an hour ago. The clothes matched and even his watch was visible on his left wrist.

"That's our victim," she said.

She scanned ahead, going faster now that they'd seen their victim but slowing down here and there as people started to crowd around the back of the boat as more and more passengers stepped on. They saw their victim once more by the time Palmer came to his final count. It turned out that Jefferson had been very close in his estimation; ninety-four people were on the *Whistlin' Pig* when it coasted out into the river on Sunday afternoon.

And one of them was the killer.

"Excuse me," Jefferson said, stepping in beside them. "I do hate to be a bother, but we need to start letting passengers on. We'll be taking off in twenty minutes. You're welcome to stay on board, maybe catch the route for yourself."

"And this will be the same route you took Sunday afternoon?"

"Yes."

Camille and Palmer shared a quick look and then a nod. "Yeah," Palmer said. "I think we'll take you up on that."

It was a good idea to see the routes and potential sights of interest along the way, though Camille hated to think they'd be wasting all of that time. Then again, they had a face now, a video clip they could pass around. Maybe taking the final trip their victim took would prove more helpful than she realized.

CHAPTER EIGHT

Camille found the ride to be very sparse, and the water was gentle and peaceful. As Camille and Palmer settled down on the topside sitting area, still using Jefferson's phone to view the footage of Sunday's ride, they were told by the captain—who finally introduced himself as Sal Miller—that there were only fifty-two people on board.

In terms of scenery, the ride didn't offer much. There were a few businesses and landmarks of note, but this was not the sort of riverboat tour that called out every single thing they passed. Instead, it seemed to be a much more laid-back experience, constructed for those that just wanted to be out on the water, away from the hassle and noise of everyday life. Camille noted that a great deal of those on board looked to be over fifty. She saw three couples that were *at least* seventy.

"Okay, so we see our guy just one more time," Palmer said. He'd taken the phone for a bit, just to give Camille's eyes a rest. "He's right here, walking by. The boat has been on the river for about half an hour by this time. But if you check here, and then the other time right before the boat pulls off, and then when he gets on…there doesn't seem to be anyone trailing him."

"So other than the fact that we've spotted him and confirmed without a doubt that he was on this boat on Sunday between three and three-fifty in the afternoon, we have nothing."

"Well, he's a bit of a slob. We do have that."

"How do you mean?"

"Right here, in this bit I just found, you can see him chewing some gum. He pops it in his mouth and when he's done with the wrapper, he just tosses it overboard, right into the river."

Camille looked to the footage and saw this. He didn't even seem to care if anyone saw him. He started chewing the gum, tossed the wrapper over into the water without a thought and then continued on his way. He walked slowly and with purpose, leaning slightly on the rail.

"You see that?" Camille asked.

"See what?"

"Does it look like he's stumbling a bit? Maybe a little lazy on his feet?"

Palmer scanned back on the footage a bit and watched as the man leaned on the rail and continued forward on shaky legs. "You think he was drinking?" Palmer asked.

"That or he just didn't have his sea legs. Or river legs…or whatever. I wonder if the bartender working right now is the same one that was on shift on Sunday."

They got up together and walked over to the bar area. It was slightly shy of noon and there were only five people sitting at the bar. The bartender was chatting with two of them—one of the older couples Camille had spotted earlier. The bartender knew they were on board and that they were FBI agents, but they had not yet spoken to him. But when he saw them approach, he held eye contact with Camille, as if sensing that his time was coming.

When Camille and Palmer approached the bar on the other side and elected to stand, not sit, the bartender wrapped up his conversation quickly but politely and then came walking over to them.

"Agents, how are you? Palmer and…Green, was it?"

"Grace," Camille corrected. "I'm curious…were you bartending on this boat on Sunday?"

"Sure was."

"I wonder if I show you a picture of a man if you might be able to remember him?"

The bartender shrugged and gave a grin that Camille found very charming It was the sort of grin that showed flawless teeth and a little dimple in his right cheek. It was a smile that had surely netted him lots of tips in the past. "Maybe. I do see a lot of folks week in and week out, though."

"How about this fellow?" Camille asked, turning Jefferson's phone so he could see the picture of their first victim.

He looked for only two or three seconds before nervously chuckling. "Oh, him. Yeah, I remember him. Talked quite a bit and had a lot to drink. He drank it all pretty quickly, though."

"Did he cause any problems?"

"Not really. He did get a little loud and I think he was just…well, you know…sort of obnoxious by default you know?"

"So if he drank, he had to run a tab with you, right?" Palmer asked.

"Most do, but if I remember correctly, he paid drink by drink."

"So there's a credit card record to trace him back here, right?"

"That's right. You may want to even talk to Mr. Jefferson about that. I'm not one hundred percent sure how that works, but if he still has merchant copies of the receipts, you could probably get a name pretty easily. If not—"

"If not, we'll have to put in an official request to the credit card company," Camille said. "And that's going to present a bunch of unnecessary obstacles. Would you happen to know what he was drinking?"

"I do, actually. He started with two mojitos and then had a few shots of bourbon. I remember because someone teased him about it…in a good natured away. Talking about how those two things would *not* mix well."

"Any idea if this man was here alone?" Palmer asked.

"Not sure, but I never saw him with anyone. He spoke to a few people here at the bar, but no one really paid him much attention."

"So no altercations or arguments with anyone? Nothing like that?"

"Not that I saw. But I do think he got yelled at by someone else—another of the crew members—for tossing trash overboard."

Palmer took Jefferson's phone back and gave the bartender a courteous nod. "Thanks for your help. Any idea where we might find Mr. Jefferson?"

"Probably the captain's quarters downstairs."

Heading back downstairs, that's exactly where they found him. Jefferson was speaking to Sal Miller, who stood by the helm but was not actively steering. They'd been chatting about something but came to a stop when Camille and Palmer entered.

"Any luck?" Jefferson asked.

"We think so," Camille said. "And your bartender was a big help. He recalls the man we're trying to identify, right down to what he had to drink. So we're hoping you have access to your merchant copies of receipts from Sunday. If we can get our hands on those, we'll likely be able to identify the victim."

Jefferson thought about it for a moment, his eyebrows arching when he realized that he would actually be able to help. "Of course, I don't have them on me, but a simple call to my office and I think I can help you. I don't keep paper copies beyond a day or so, but I have digital records of all credit card purchases related to the sale of alcohol for up to three months."

"Perfect."

"And it shouldn't take long," he said. "I'll do the whole thing on speaker."

He stepped away from Miller and the trio collected in the rear of the small room that made up the captain's quarters. Jefferson placed a call that was answered on the second ring. "Sunny Day Tours, this is Rita."

"Rita, it's Christopher. You busy right now?"

"Not at this moment, no, sir."

"Go into the books and pull up all credit card purchases at the bar of the *Whistlin' Pig* last Sunday, would you?"

"Sure thing," she said.

As they waited for Rita to speak up again, Jefferson covered the mouthpiece and looked to Camille. "What was the guy drinking?"

"Mojitos and bourbon. And apparently, it was all in a pretty short window of time. He also didn't keep a tab. Your bartender said he kept paying for each drink individually, as if he really didn't plan to drink too much."

They waited in silence, the boat rolling right along as they waited for Rita again. It didn't take long, and when she same back she sounded quite pleased with herself that she'd been able to come up with the information so quickly.

"I've got those transactions up," she announced. "You looking for anything in particular?"

"Yeah, actually. I need you to find the same card number paying for individual drinks. Mojitos and shots of bourbon. Not one tab altogether, but each drink separately."

"Shouldn't be too hard. Looks like that was a slow afternoon," Rita said, mostly just mumbling to herself. And then: "Yeah, here we are. Same card, purchasing one, two, three mojitos and two shots of bourbon."

"What's the name on the card?" Jefferson asked.

"Kevin Pleasant, from what I see here."

"That's perfect, Rita. Thanks so much."

It sounded as if Rita was about to say something else, but Jefferson ended the call before she could get anything else out. "Was that what you needed?" Jefferson asked.

"That's an enormous help, yes," Camille said, already pulling out her phone.

While she was not yet quite familiar enough with the people and offices in the New Orleans field office, she had programmed a number into her phone that would take her directly to records and research. She placed the call and, in a quick and efficient conversation, asked a monotone man on the other line to pull up records for Kevin Pleasant.

As the man worked, the sound of his fingers typing barely audible through the phone, Camille received another call as signified by the click-and-beep noise in her ear.

"Hold on a second," she told the man in records. "I've got an incoming call." She switched over and said: "This is Agent Grace."

"Hello there, Agent Grace," said a quiet male voice. "This is Deputy Jack Henson, New Orleans PD. I just spoke with our assistant director and he told me to call you."

"Okay. What can I do for you?"

"Well, you probably should come over to Bywater. We found another body in the river."

CHAPTER NINE

Palmer had seen bodies pulled from bodies of water before—two from the Mississippi River long before Camille Grace had ever come to New Orleans. And though he'd seen it enough times to not be shocked, there was still something unnerving about it. Even now, watching as the State Police dragged the body of a woman from underneath a mossy dock, it unnerved him. The limp state of the body, the way everything was soaked—it reminded him far too much of hauling a fish out of the river.

The five policemen on the scene stepped aside to allow Palmer and Camille to observe the body. On the water, the little aluminum boat with the outboard motor idled while the two policemen on board continued to scan the water, looking for anything the woman may have incidentally left behind.

Palmer stood slightly to the side as Camille drew closer to the body and knelt down by it on the dock. The woman looked to be in her forties, pretty in a plain sort of way. Her black hair looked almost like oil, soaked and strewn about in a limp sort of array on the wooden dock. Behind them, a few more policemen were speaking with homeowners that had a view of the river and the dock from their massive back yards. Their houses, likely in the very high six figures, if not in the low seven figures, loomed behind them, as if judging the scene.

"This is a very recent murder," Camille said. "Look at the neck."

Palmer had seen it as soon as Camille mentioned it. There was a clear indication that the woman had been strangled. Not only was there a raw sort of rubbing along the base of her neck, but there was a ring-shaped bruise as well. And the bruise was fresh, still forming slightly in color and size.

"Does anyone have anything I can reach into her pockets with?" Camille asked.

One of the police officers stepped forward—it was one of the men that had pulled the body from the river. He was fumbling around in his front pocket, eventually pulling out a very small workman's tool. He opened it up, snapped up the small pliers fixture, and handed it to

Camille.

"Thanks," she said, instantly angling in toward the dead woman's front pocket. Palmer watched her work, the moment standing out as another example of how hands-on and unapologetic she could be when it came to the cases she worked. She was never rude or aggressive when it came to claiming her place in the hierarchy but still somehow always come off as being the one in charge. This didn't really bother Palmer, as she seemed to be an exceptional agent, but every now and then he had to remind himself not to be so passive.

"Looking for another ticket?" he asked.

"Yes," she said, digging the pliers in and moving them around slowly, carefully. "And here we are," she said. She pressed down on the handle of the workman's tool and pulled the pliers out. A ticket stub that looked almost identical to the one found in Kevin Pleasant's pocket was pinched between the teeth. When she set it on the dock beside the woman, Palmer could see that there were minor differences, though.

First of all, the name of the boat was different—though it was a name he'd seen and heard very recently. "*Wheeler's Delight*," he said, reading it out loud.

"And it's a ticket from this morning," Camille said, pointing to the date. "Jesus, Palmer…this woman hasn't been dead for any more than four hours."

"And this is the second body to come off *Wheeler's Delight* in less than forty-eight hours. If we—"

"Hey, agents?"

They turned to the voice, coming from the boat still searching the water. It had pulled over to the bank and one of the officers was reaching into the water with a metal rod with pinchers on the end. They'd found something.

"What is it?" Camille asked.

The man with the rod held up what he found. It was a small purse, the kind that was built to look cute and stylish rather than serve any real purpose like holding more than five or six items. The driver backed away from the bank and came over to the dock, just twenty or so feet away. Palmer reached over across the water and took it from him.

He peered inside and saw that everything was matching the other two victims so far. The woman's wallet was inside, as was her cellphone. Camille reached into the purse and plucked out the wallet, carefully holding it only by the edges. When she opened it, they found two credit cards and thirty-three dollars in cash, completely soaked.

Again, this murder had not been with the intention of robbery.

At the front of the wallet was a clear plastic sleeve where the woman's driver's license was stored. Her name was Natania Whitehead and she was a local. Her birthdate placed her as being forty-three years old.

"Natania Whitehead," Palmer announced to the cops. "Can someone get on this, maybe see if there's family we need to inform?"

There was the sound of motion and movement behind them as the cops responded to his request. But after a few seconds, there were footsteps on the dock behind them. Palmer turned and saw a cop coming towards them. He looked a bit confused, maybe even hesitant. "You…you said Natania Whitehead?" he asked.

"That's right. Why? You know her?"

"No, but I know the name, I heard it this morning down at the station. She called in to see what she could do about filing a police report."

"A report against who?" Camille asked.

"One of the waiters on the…on the riverboat she was riding this morning."

Palmer could feel the stir of electricity in the air at this revelation. Camille's sudden, rigid posture told him that she felt it too. Hell, even the cop seemed to sense it, too.

"Did you take the call?" Palmer asked.

"No, but I got the basic information. She complained that one of the waiters was getting handsy with her. She said when she asked to speak to the manager, there was no manager on board. She went to the captain to complain about it, but he didn't seem to give a damn. So she called the police."

"Did anyone respond?" Camille asked.

"That, I don't know. I can call and find out. But I mean, if she was *on* the boat, there would be nothing we could do until she got off. I'd imagine someone took the report and asked her to come to the station to properly file the report if she was serious about it."

"Don't sweat it," Camille said. "Give me the name of who I need to contact at your precinct, and we'll take it from there."

But the officer already held out his phone and started placing the call. He handed it over to Camille and said, "Ask for Griffey. They'll know everything."

After two more rings, the phone was answered by a loud male voice with a thick, southern accent. Camille set the phone to speaker to allow

Palmer to listen in. "Yeah, this is Griffey."

"Hello, this is Agent Camille Grace, with the FBI. I'm currently on the banks of the Mississippi, looking at what I believe is the third victim of a potential serial killer. Her name is Natania Whitehead, and I believe she called in this morning to file a report about a waiter on a riverboat."

"Ah, that she did. Yeah, I took that call."

"And do you have a name on the waiter?"

"Maybe. She said all she got from his name tag was *Roger.* I called the riverboat company, gave them the name and the name of the boat, and they said the only Roger they had working that particular boat—*Wheeler's Delight*—is a Roger Keenan. I've got a unit on the way over to meet with the boat's captain right now. Seems the owner of the company is very hard to get in touch with."

"Does Roger Keenan have a record?" Camille asked.

"He does. Nothing recent, though. It's all from at least four years ago. One report of drunk and disorderly, and another for assault."

"Do me a favor and call your unit off," she said. "Me and my partner would like to speak with him. Also, if you don't mind, can you call the riverboat company back and find out if Roger Keenan was also working Sunday night?"

"No need. I've got his schedule right here, for the past month. And yes…he was working as a waiter on Wheeler's Delight on Sunday night."

Palmer watched a little spark of excitement spring up in Camille's eyes. He looked away. Quickly, though. Lingering on looks like that from an already attractive Camille Grace was the sort of thing that caused crushes to develop.

"Thanks for your help, officer," Camille said. "One last thing: where was your unit headed in order to meet with Roger and the captain?"

"Hold one sec…I can get that address."

As they waited, Palmer looked back down at the dead woman—to Natania Whitehead. She hadn't been robbed, she was fully clothed, and she did not appear to have been beaten before she was strangled and tossed overboard. And assuming all three victims so far—Natania Whitehead, Brittany Gable, and Kevin Pleasant—were connected, that meant three victims in the span of about five days.

So while it was indeed exciting to have such a lead, all of this sat heavy on Palmer. It meant they had a killer that was driven and motivated. And if it turned out the waiter wasn't their killer, that could mean trouble. Because if they didn't find out what was motivating him, there would likely be another victim very soon.

CHAPTER TEN

Wheeler's Delight was much larger and grander than the *Whistlin' Pig,* but Camille barely took the time to admire the look and feel of the boat. After she and Palmer discreetly showed their badges to the woman at the ticket office, they slipped right into the flow of people that were lined up to get on board for the 1:30 excursion. Some were already heading to the bar area, located on the lower deck while others were taking their time to walk around the boat, taking in the sights.

While this was not an undercover job by any stretch of the imagination, it did *feel* like it to Camille. It was more than just trying to catch a potential suspect unaware, but also trying to fit in with an accumulating crowd as the time for *Wheeler's Delight* to depart neared. They made no rush, no sudden moved to hunt down the waiter in question, Roger Keenan. Instead, they moved through the crowd as if they were normal travelers, out for a relaxing afternoon on the river.

They took the time to take a loop around the first-floor deck, waiting for the boat to get moving before they made their way up to the second deck, where the café was located. It was a large café, but not big enough to be considered a restaurant. Camille recalled Brittany's friends talking about the buffet, of how Brittany had maybe had too many crawfish or shrimp. There was a long table against the far left wall; Camille assumed it was the table that a good portion of the buffet had been set out on.

A few people were taking their places at other tables. From what Camille could see, it was very much a first-come-first-serve situation. A small, thin woman was pouring coffee for the few people that had come to the café while three other staff members were huddled near the back, looking over a menu and glancing out to the tables. There were two men and another woman, all dressed in very plain black and white uniforms. Of the men, one was quite young, surely no older than twenty-five or so. The other was a handsome thirty-something. His black hair was slicked back and put up in a short ponytail.

Palmer noticed the trio first and started slowly making his way over in their direction. Camille did the same, still trying not to seem too obvious. As they neared the back, where the trio of employees were standing, Camille put on an act of looking out of the windows, glaring down to the Mississippi as it rolled by. As she turned to Palmer, pretending to chatter with him about something, she looked back over to the three crew members. The man with the ponytail was turned in her direction, but still looking down at either a menu or a table seating chart. But she was able to see his nametag—to see that it read *Roger.*

"There's our suspect," she said under her breath. "See the nametag?"

"Yeah, I see him," Palmer said. "Let's go say hello."

Slowly giving up their ruse second by second, they made a direct line for the three employees. The woman of the group had already started to distance herself taking a stack of menus with her to distribute out among the tables.

As they approached the two men, apparently waiters given their attire and the fact that they were discussing menus and tables in the café, Camille noticed how Palmer subtly glided right in front of her. It was a protective thing, a professional way of being chivalrous that she appreciated. If anyone other than Palmer had done it just for the sake of old-fashioned tropes, she would have likely been irritated.

"Roger?" Palmer said as they closed in on the two waiters. "Roger Keenan?"

When the waiter looked up, Camille could see the practiced smile on his face, the smile he was supposed to use when interacting with any guest on the boat. But when he took a moment to actually take a good look at them, the smile went away. She even caught him looking quickly to their waists, past Palmer's jacket, specifically. He was looking for guns, for any sign that they were here with law enforcement.

When he saw the bit of Palmer's Glock revealed beneath the jacket, Roger Keenan backed away. He pushed the other waiter aside and hustled to the swinging door on the backside of the room, almost directly behind him.

"Well, at least he's taking the guesswork out of it," Palmer said as he took off, chasing after him.

Camille also fell in line and they both went pushing through the swinging door just four or five seconds behind Roger Keenan.

The swinging door led through a small kitchen area, and a door immediately to the right, which was only now just swinging closed from Keenan having passed through it, led out into the open air of the second deck's primary walkway. Camille caught sight of Keenan for just a second as he came to the end of the walkway and dashed hard to the left. Someone out of their line of sight let out a yell—it was filled with terror for a moment and was then cut off by a splashing noise.

When Camille and Palmer came to the end of the walkway and to the larger, open area at the front of the boat, Camille saw where a small group was gathered by the side, just a few feet away from the front of the boat.

"Hey!" someone yelled, looked around for help. "Hey, some lady just fell over! She was pushed!"

"Who did it?" Camille yelled to the group. "Which way did he go?"

Two people instantly pointed to the set of stairs just off to the right. The stairs led up to the third and final deck. Even as she looked toward the stairway, she could just barely see Keenan reaching the top. She looked back at the people looking out into the river at the woman that had been pushed overboard, not wanting to just leave her. But then she saw one of the crew members of *Wheeler's Delight*. It was a young woman, rushing over with a life jacket in one hand and lifebuoy in the other.

Assuming that particular emergency was taken care of, she bounded up the stairs with Palmer still leading the way. A few people were coming down, causing Camille to have to lean tight against the rail. Before they reached the top, she could hear a man from the third deck yelling out a string of curse words. Someone else let out a surprised cry.

They came to the top of the stairs and saw a canopied third floor, complete with a small bar and, near the back, a concave structure that held three restrooms. Camille watched as a rushing figure made its way into the center one, slamming the door behind them. She hadn't seen for certain that it was Roger Keenan, but she figured it was a safe enough bet. They ran across the floor, dodging a few people that were sipping on drinks and in the middle of conversations.

"The guy's got to be an idiot, right" Palmer said. "Locking himself in a bathroom."

Camille only shrugged as Palmer knocked on the door. "Mr. Keenan, my name is Agent Scott Palmer, with the FBI. If you open the door now, I may be convinced to forget that you just made me run around a riverboat."

There was no response at first but then a voice on the other side of the door spoke up. "What do you even want, man?"

"Juts to talk. That's it. Your name came up in an investigation we're working on."

“Nah, man, I’m not coming out.”

“You don’t really have much of a choice,” Palmer responded. “I don’t mind kicking the door down. But if I do that, I’m going to be mad. And then you’re going to be arrested. But if you open up now, I can maybe get you off of this boat *not* in handcuffs. You’ve got five seconds to decide.”

After two seconds, the toilet flushed from inside the bathroom. Immediately after that, the door opened and Roger Keenan stepped out. He did his very best to appear as if he had not been rattled by the past three minutes or so.

“What’s up?” Keenan asked.

“What’s up is that we need to ask you a few questions. You work on the boat…where can we talk in private?”

“There’s a small break room,” Keenan said. Camille thought he looked very nervous under his calm exterior. It showed through because he was trying a little *too* hard to seem as if he wasn’t bothered by any of this.

“Then lead the way,” Camille said, stepping aside and wondering *why* he was playing it so cool. She noticed that Palmer held a steady hand on Keenan’s arm just in case he tried to make a run for it. Keenan seemed not to care but he was still somehow very rigid. It made her wonder if he was hiding something and if, within the next half an hour or so, they might discover that accidentally pushing a woman into the river while running away from federal agents might be the least of his concerns.

CHAPTER ELEVEN

"So what did you flush down the toilet before you came out?" Camille asked.

Roger Keenan's face crumpled into a look of disgust. He clearly hadn't liked that question. The three of them were sitting in a very small breakroom, decorated with only a bit of counter space, a single, small table, and a microwave.

"You know, my manager is going to know I'm missing anytime now," Keenan said.

"Not our problem," Palmer said. "Now, answer Agent Grace. What were you flushing?"

"Pot."

"You smoked recently?"

Keenan sighed and then shrugged, as if he really didn't see where he'd done anything wrong. "After my first shift. So what?"

"Your first shift," Camille said. "So you were working on *Wheeler's Delight* for the morning excursion, too, right?"

"Yeah, I was." He gave them a hard, calculated look that then softened with a bit of realization. "Hold on. Is this about that crazy woman that said I was hitting on her?"

"It is," Camille said. "We know that she claims you made advances to her and when she tried to complain about it, no one took her seriously. She called the cops to see if they would do anything about it."

A little flicker of fear crossed his face. "She called the cops?"

"She did."

"But you two are with the FBI?"

Camille showed him her badge and ID, plopping them both down on the table. "We are. And we'd like to hear your side of the story."

Keenan still seemed legitimately confused that the FBI would be involved in a little potential sexual harassment, but he did his best to go on as, bit by bit, that fabricated cool exterior started to crumble.

"Well, part of my job is to be polite…friendly. This lady, she came in and just ordered coffee and a bagel. Or a donut. I don't remember which. I was just asking her what she had planned for the day and we were chatting, you know. I put my hand on her shoulder and you would have thought I'd cupped her between the legs. I mean, she lost it. I apologized and everything, man. Gave her the coffee and her donut or whatever for free. She sat at the table for another five minutes, asked for another waiter. I heard she'd complained about me, but…shit, man. I had no idea it was *that* bad."

"Let me ask you something else," Camille said. "This past Saturday, did you have any sort of arguments or events similar to the one you had with the woman this morning?"

He took a moment to think it through and actually smiled a bit when he shook his head. "No. I mean, there was a small bachelorette party on here Saturday night. Some of the girls got tipsy and started talking to me…sort of flirting, you know? I flirted back, but nothing out of the ordinary. And no one complained. In fact, it all sort of came to an end for them when they realized one of their friends was missing."

"So you recall that moment?" Palmer asked. "When the woman went missing?"

"Yeah," Keenan said, finally beginning to understand that there was more going on here than a simple check-in about a report filed against him earlier in the day. "Hey, what the hell is going on here?"

Palmer looked over to Camille and she gave him a nod—a sign to go ahead and reveal their hand. She wasn't quite sure if she bought the act yet, but the next few seconds would tell.

"The woman that went missing on Saturday night," Palmer said, "was named Brittany Gable. Her body was found yesterday along the banks of the river.

"Oh…oh, Jesus. That's terrible."

"The woman that filed the complaint against you this morning was named Natania Whitehead. Her body was found in the river less than two hours ago."

Keenan's face went pale, his eyes blinking rapidly has he processed it. For a moment, Camille thought he might legitimately get sick. "Are you serious right now?"

"We are," Camille said. "And as I'm sure you *must* understand, the fact that she tried to file a complaint against you does seem suspicious. And *that's* why we wanted to speak with you."

Any semblance of control dissolved from Keenan's expression at this revelation. "You think I killed her? Just because she reported me? Are you…are you *kidding?*"

He was on his feet now, glaring down at them. Palmer stood up as well, making a calm-down gesture with his hands. "Look at the picture it paints, Mr. Keenan. Of course we had to at least consider it. But you said you were working, right?"

"Right."

"Can you have anyone back that up? Was there *anyone* or even a few people that would have seen you for the duration of the ride after Natania Whitehead left the table?"

"Well, yeah. Yeah…at least two other waiters. And there was this older guy…a really old man, with a Vietnam Veteran hat on. I talked to him for at least the last fifteen minutes or so of the trip. He was telling me about his time overseas. I don't know if you can get his name, but…"

"And what about Saturday night? After it was discovered that Brittany Gable was missing, how did the rest of your night go?"

"I mean, it put a damper on everyone's night, you know? But I kept working. Serving tables, even stepped in and helped at the bar for a little while."

"And there are people that can back that up?"

"Yeah, a ton of folks. The bartender, three or four other waiters and waitresses, probably the hostess, too. We had a buffet that night, so we had a girl standing in as hostess to make sure the place wasn't stacked. I checked in with her every couple of minutes."

The more potential alibis and witnesses to his whereabouts he mentioned, the less convinced Camille was that he was their man.

"Is this the only riverboat you work on, Mr. Keenan?" Palmer asked.

"No. I also sometimes work on the New Orleans Queen."

"Is that boat also owned by River Runners?"

"Yeah, it is."

"Have you ever been on a smaller boat called the *Whistlin' Pig*? Not just for work, but as a passenger?"

Keenan shook his head "No. I don't…I don't think I've ever heard of it. Besides, man, the only riverboats I've ever stepped foot on are ones I've worked on."

"Mr. Keenan," Camille said, "if we were to ask for your whereabouts last Sunday, when there was another murder on a smaller boat, would you be able to provide proof?"

"Sunday…yeah, well, I slept in. I always sleep in on Sunday. Didn't get out of the apartment until about one or two. Went and saw movie with this girl I'm seeing, then went for an early dinner. After that, I met up with my brother to go see this weird little Indie band down near the French Quarter."

Camille nodded, all but sure now that this was not their killer. A woman, a brother, a band that would require tickets to see…it would be far too easy to find out if he was being truthful. And given the way his personality had changed when he'd realized the severity of why they were questioning him, she had no doubt he *was* being truthful.

"Thanks for your time, Mr. Keenan," she said. "We'll likely be asking the captain or the company's owner for video footage. But in the meantime, if you hear of anything from any of the other employees, I'd appreciate it if you'd call us immediately."

"Yeah, I can do that," he said, still slightly dazed.

When Camille and Palmer got back to their feet, Keenan also stood. He seemed out of it, processing all he'd just heard.

"I…I, uh…am I good to get back to work?"

"Yes," Palmer said, handing him a business card. "And like Agent Grace said…don't hesitate to call if anything pops up. And maybe talk to your manager; you did, after all, accidentally push someone off the boat."

Keenan pocketed the card and left the agents alone in the break room. Camille looked at Palmer and he shook his head. "Well, possession of marijuana seems to be about the *only* thing he's guilty of. Any ideas?"

She had one, but she hated to go there so soon. Records and searching for links, digging through files and background information. It was a necessity but always made her feel as if she was wasting time.

"Records, right?" he said with a defeated grin.

"How'd you know?"

"That sad, sad look on your face."

She opened the door and let him out first. "You're starting to know me a little too well, Palmer."

"Is that a bad thing?" he said, smiling.

"I honestly don't know yet," she said, closing the break room door behind her and already focusing her mind on how to best search for links between the three victims.

CHAPTER TWELVE

The bad part about killing that last woman so early in the day was that it left an entire day spread out before him. Not only that, but the more he killed, the easier it became. There had been three so far—and the last two had come less than two days apart. Hell, the third woman—the one that had been feeding the donut to the ducks—hadn't even been planned. But the opportunity had presented itself and he'd just been unable to resist.

It was so easy. And it seemed to be getting easier.

But even now, as he walked along Canal Street, he could see that there was still much work to be done. There were old fliers and miniature posters in the gutters, candy and snack wrappers on the sidewalks. And seeing it all, one discarded flier caught his attention. He leaned down, picked it up, and read over it. The large letters at the top read: **Caterwaul Bass Tournament!**

"Almost forgot about that," he said under his breath. And right away, a very specific face came to mind.

It was a woman he was familiar with. A woman he had warned before he'd come to understand that he could actually do something about the way people behaved. Before he knew he could correct them for good.

He supposed he understood the allure of fishing. The sport and the patience of it all. He could even respect the sport and the excitement of a tournament. But he had seen what those tournaments left behind. Small and big tournaments alike, the participants and the fans had no respect for the land, no sense of pride. They left litter behind in the form of Styrofoam cups, little plastic buckets that had once contained bait, beer cans, bottles, snack wrappers. It was awful.

He read the details along the bottom. The tournament was to occupy a thirty mile stretch of the river, a special section that had been specifically reserved for the event, though participants were welcome to venture out to their own favorite places, so long as they were back at the ceremonial dock by six that afternoon.

A grin crept across his face. That woman…that stubborn woman. He'd seen her twice last year and once just a few weeks ago. She had a favorite spot for sure. He'd seen her there on each of those occasions, not too far away from where he lived, in fact. And hadn't she mentioned something to him about the tournament that last time he spoke to her? Oh, he'd tried to remain nice, tried to keep his calm as she'd flicked her cigarette butt out into the water. He'd tried to pretend it hadn't bothered him when she'd purposefully spilled out the last little bit of her warm, flat soda into the river.

She'd even boasted about how that sport was her favorite spot—her magic trick.

So why *wouldn't* she use it to snag a few fish for her tournament.

With the same smile on his face, he crammed the flier into his pants pocket, turned around, and made his way back to his truck. It was still parked in the lot just two blocks over from where *Wheeler's Delight* had set sail from earlier in the day.

He thought of that woman, complaining about something on her phone while she poisoned the ducks with her donuts. She'd never seen it coming. He'd worked fast—so fast that he hadn't been able to properly choke her out. When he'd flung her overboard, he was quite sure her neck had snapped. He supposed he'd find out either on the evening news or tomorrow's paper.

When he came to his truck fifteen minutes later and started the engine, he was whistling a happy little tune. He had a busy day ahead of him after all.

And to start it all off, he had a fishing tournament to get to.

CHAPTER THIRTEEN

It was a refreshing change of pace to be working a case within the city limits. It allowed Camille to do her records and research digging in the semi-comfort of her own office. It had not yet *quite* started to feel like a home away from home, but it was a place she was starting to feel comfortable. Even when Palmer joined her, following her down to the basement level without being invited or asking to come along, she felt secure. It was a space of her own, and she was slowly growing used to it.

"I'm still not sure why they stuck you in the basement," Palmer said as he sat on the little loveseat she'd pushed into the back corner. "You know there's plenty of extra office space upstairs."

"Is there, really?" she asked. "I thought you were in a cubicle."

"A cubicle is an office," he said.

"I beg to differ. I much prefer the isolation of the basement."

"Does that mean you want me out of here?"

"Did I say that?" she asked as she logged onto the bureau network.

"It was implied. Hey, hold on I'll run and get my laptop. Want me to grab some lunch while I'm up there?"

"What's up there?"

"A bit of everything."

"Sure. Surprise me."

He left, leaving her with yet another feeling of familiarity and ease. She and Palmer were getting comfortable with one another, the back and forth banter coming more naturally every time they spent time together. It was more than just that they interacted well with one another, though. He was good agent, took no crap from suspects, and had a level head on his shoulders. He was also chivalrous, but in a professional way that had never made her feel awkward or that he believed she was helpless.

It was a good state of mind to be in as she started looking in the bureau database for information on their three victims. It took a while to find them because as it turned out, the very few dings on their records were minor—and Natania Whitehead had none at all. The only thing Camille could determine about the three victims was that they were very different from one another.

Different ages, different occupations, varied races, different genders. There seemed to be nothing to link these three, other than the fact they had been on a riverboat just before the murderer took their lives.

As she printed the files out for easier access and comparison, Palmer came back into the office. He was carrying microwave containers in each hand and had a bottle of water under each arm.

"You a fan of pho?"

"Not sure. I only had it once, and it wasn't microwavable."

She took the lunch and sat it on her desk. Palmer reclaimed his spot on the loveseat and looked over at what she had pulled up on her screen. The printer hummed to the right as it spit out the files.

"Anything of note?" he asked.

"Nothing at all…other than how very different these victims are."

She slurped up some of the noodles from the container, finding it surprisingly good. "We've got a young woman at a bachelorette party that works as a receptionist at a graphic design company, then a forty-something man that worked as a brick layer, and then, as of this morning, a forty-something African American woman that worked at an OBGYN's office. I don't know if you can get any more varied than that."

"You think he' just attacking randomly?" Palmer asked. "Whenever the mood strikes, whenever he finds it convenient?"

"Could be. And he's clearly choosing riverboats as his killing grounds. Which seems very strange in and of itself."

As Palmer reached out for one of the printouts, Camille was distracted by the buzzing of her phone. When she looked at the caller ID and saw that it was Deanna, she almost ignored it. But then she wondered if it might be related to her father. A father that had stubbornly refused treatment for his colon cancer for almost a year.

"Sorry," she told Palmer as she made her way to the door. "I have to take this. But you keep looking. Make yourself at home."

He nodded, stretched out, and kicked his feet up on the other end of the loveseat. Camille stepped out, closing the door behind her and walking out into the small hallway beyond. She answered, not sure of what to expect from the other end.

"Hey, Deanna." She figured calling her by her entire name and not just as *D*, as she had since childhood, might help set the tone without her having to be so blatant.

"Hey, Camille. Is this a good time? Do you have a few minutes?"

"Not really, but it's as good a time as any."

"Okay. I'll keep it short, then. Look…I spoke with your father on the phone yesterday. He said something came up in conversation when the two of you spoke last. About Nanette. And I feel like I need to apologize."

"I feel that way, too. But I keep trying to tell myself you weren't keeping secrets on purpose."

"I wasn't. I swear. Honestly, your father has been so scatterbrained over the years that I was never sure what you knew and what you didn't. He and I have always kept in touch but as you know, he's not the best when it comes to communication. Especially if it involves relational stuff."

"Well, what do *you* know, Deanna?"

"What do you mean?"

"I mean about Nanette," Camille snapped. "That time you saw her twelve years ago…have you seen her since?"

"No."

"Have you heard from her?"

There was a slight pause on the other end and when Deanna did finally speak up, her. voice was soft and on edge. "There was just one single letter. From about five or six years ago."

Camille felt as if the floor had been yanked out from under her. She leaned against the wall to steady herself. "Where did the letter come from?"

"In the letter, she said she was in Juarez, Mexico."

Words would not come to her. She was elated, excited, and furious. She wanted to ask more questions, to beg Deanna to tell her everything she knew. But she also didn't want to come off as begging or weak.

"I can't do this right now. I have to…D, I have a case I'm working on. A pretty pressing one, at that. Can we talk about this later?"

"Yes. And I'd actually…I'd actually like that. Maybe you can come over for dinner. I know you've been in the city for almost a month now, but have you really gotten to experience that good old southern hospitality in its truest form?"

"Hospitality," Camille said, mocking. "You've kept secrets. You've…never mind. I'll call you when this is over and we'll set something up. I have to go."

She ended the call and reached for the door to her office when one single remark Deanna had made rung out like a bell in her head.

...but have you really gotten to experience that good old southern hospitality in its truest form?

Southern hospitality. Something about it hooked her thoughts, trying to sink itself into the case. She finally opened the door and stepped inside, her thoughts suddenly leaping all over the place.

"You okay?" Palmer asked.

"Yeah, I'm fine. Palmer…the waiter, Roger Keenan. He said the bachelorette party was being loud and sort of wild, right?"

"Not in those words, but yes."

"And with the first victim, Kevin Pleasant, remember, on the footage we saw, he was tossing a bit of trash over the rail, into the river. A gum wrapper, I believe."

"Yeah, that's right," Palmer said.

Southern hospitality...

It felt like a stretch, but she wondered if they might find some sort of slight offense in the way Natania Whitehead had spent her morning.

"You got something?" Palmer asked.

"I don't know. I think I do want to call the manager or maybe someone on staff on *Wheeler's Delight* this morning to see if anyone saw Natania Whitehead do anything that might be seen as disrespectful."

"It's a trail worth sniffing out, I guess. You think the killer is acting as some sort of social police or something?"

"I'm not sure. Seems possible, though."

She took out her phone and called the management offices for River Runners. It took two more calls to different individuals, but she was finally connected with someone that was currently working on the boat. It was an assistant manager for the company, a gravel-voice woman named Betsy. She placed the call on speaker mode so Palmer could listen in.

"Ma'am, my name is Camille Grace, an agent with the FBI here at the New Orleans field office. We're trying to dig up some information on a woman that was on *Wheeler's Delight* this morning. Her name is Natania Whitehead and she had made complaints about one of your waiters—Roger Keenan."

"Oh, yeah. Her. I remember."

"What exactly do you remember?"

"Well, she tried convincing a few staff members that Roger had come on to her. No one really took her seriously because a few others actually saw the altercation. After that, when she was given the number of our manager, she went up to the main deck to call him. Someone else, one of the custodians, said they heard her sort of whispering into the phone, complaining about Roger. Said she was sort of absently tossing breadcrumbs or a biscuit or something into the water. Or maybe it was a pastry of some kind."

"A donut, maybe?" She recalled that's what Roger had said he'd delivered to her table with her coffee.

"I honestly don't know. I can check if you need me to."

"No, that's okay. But you do know for sure she was tossing something—some sort of food—overboard?"

"Yes."

Camille and Palmer shared a glance over the phone. Weak lead or not, at least there was now another connection between the victims. They'd all been on riverboats and were partaking in activities that might seem rude or mildly offensive.

"Thanks for your help, Betsy," Camille said, ending the call.

With a grin, Palmer opened up the computer bag that had been on his shoulder—an item Camille had missed having been so deep into the records and then her conversation with Deanna.

"I'm thinking maybe someone linked with an environmental group."

"I was thinking the same thing. Or maybe just someone that doesn't like that his city has become this loud, noisy, and sometimes dirty place. That would also include loud young women at a bachelorette party."

"Either way, it gives us a few more avenues to pursue."

"Then make yourself comfortable," she said, nodding back over to the loveseat. "We may be digging for a while."

CHAPTER FOURTEEN

Within an hour, Camille and Palmer also had the assistance of a woman that worked in a remote office, dealing only with credit card and cell phone tracking. While Palmer worked with her, Camille worked with the primary management office of River Runners, trying to get as many names as she could of people that had been on board one of their riverboats in the past week.

She started by trying to work the same magic the bartender on the *Whistlin' Pig* had managed to pull off. And though it took far too many phone calls to get any results, she finally had someone working to pull credit card numbers from anyone that had purchased food or beverages over the past week.

"You understand, though," the snooty-sounding man on the other end said, "that it's going to be a deep pool of names and numbers."

"I do. And the sooner you get them to us, the sooner we can start thinning it out."

She'd always been of the mind that working diligently on phone calls and emails was more tiring than actually being out in the field. And after an hour and a half of making numerous calls and compiling information, she was starting to feel it. However, it was also around this time that the woman at the remote office started to get a few matches here and there. She had been cross-referencing credit card information pulled from River Runners with the names of passengers of both *Whistlin' Pig* and *Wheeler's Delight*, trying to find anyone that was affiliated with environmental groups. The list wasn't as big as the snooty-sounding man from River Runners had assumed. Not everyone, it seemed, was happy to drop extra money once they were on the boat. And since some people still paid cash for tickets, even when they contacted the ticket office, they were unable to get a complete list of passengers—just those that had paid with credit cards. And while it *was* the majority of the passengers, it was still not a complete list. And Camille couldn't help but think that a killer that worked so methodically might take the precaution of using cash.

Camille was in the midst of researching her twenty-second name on the database when Palmer's phone rang. He put it on speaker when he saw that it was the woman that had been helping remotely.

"So, I've got not one but *two* names for you guys," she said. "One of them, while suspicious, can be ruled out right away, though. Seems he's been in prison for the last sixteen months and was only just released two days ago."

"So he wouldn't have been on the *Whistlin' Pig* to kill Kevin Pleasant," Camille muttered.

"The second is a man named Sully Allin. Based on what I can see on his record, he's an alligator poacher. Sort of a strange business if you ask me."

"Christ, not more alligators," Palmer said.

Camille opened up a browser on her laptop and typed in the name: *Sully Allin.* The first result was to a website that seemed to promote Allin's business. As she scanned the home page copy, she read it out loud to Palmer.

"'Whether we want to admit it or not, wildlife preservation organizations aren't always the most humane solution for removing dangerous wildlife from your property. The death and harm of the wonderful creatures we share this area with are seen as just part of the job. If you find yourself wanting to rid your land of invasive or dangerous animals such as snakes, alligators, or even rabid animals in a humane manner, I'm the guy for the job.' And he has a bunch of environmental slogans and images up."

The woman on the other line spoke up again. "Well, it gets even better. Last year, he made not one, not two, but *three* complaints about the way the riverboat operations are run in New Orleans. He says many of the routes are destructive to the natural habitats of birdlife. He tried starting petitions and Facebook pages to get people to make a fuss with him but I can't see where any of it made any real difference."

"Seems pretty relevant if you ask me," Palmer said.

"Same here," Camille said. Scrolling to the bottom of the page, she said, "Oh, and look at that. Here's his contact information, complete with an address."

"Fine then," Palmer said with a sigh. "Let's go pay him a visit."

"Something wrong?"

"I had my fill of alligators with our last case. That's all."

Camille grinned, though memories of their last case came flooding back—a case where she'd come face to face with two alligators in less than two days. But thinking about that case was also a reminder of how she'd come out of it. Not only that but how she and Palmer had come to very quickly trust their instincts and the capabilities of one another.

Smiling, she grasped Palmer's shoulder. "Don't worry. I'll take the lead. I'll take care of you."

"That doesn't help," he said as they started for the door, Camille thanking the woman from records and ending the call.

They hurried to the elevators, Camile already inputting Sully Allin's address into her phone's GPS.

***

Camille was starting to wonder if Palmer's fears about facing gators again was a rational one. Sully Allin's house was located in the same sort of area they'd visited during their last case. Stretches of poorly maintained roads, overgrown fields, and tightly grown greenery bordering along everywhere. One wrong turn and you'd end up in a swamp, a desolate field, or God only knew where else.

The houses they passed were all old and in states of ruin—the porches were lopsided, there were trees growing dangerously close, and the siding had started peeling away from some, while others were stained with years of dust and mildew.

While Camille drove, Palmer was scrolling around on his phone, trying to find reviews of Allin's services. It was such a niche service and interest that it had been a fruitless search. But as they neared the last turn that would take them to Allin's home, Palmer finally found something.

"Hey, Facebook pays off again," he said. "I've got a post here from a client of Allin's. He says Allin himself seemed like a nice guy at first, but it was clear almost right away that he doesn't practice what he preaches. He had Allin come in to remove two baby gators and a mother than looked to be injured. He said Allin handled them roughly and pretty much stomped on the head of one of the babies. But then, later on, someone else comments that Allin was actually at a ticket booth to one of the riverboats several months ago. Trying to start trouble with the crew before they took off."

"Did anything happen?" Camille asked.

"It doesn't say here. But later down in the thread, Allin himself responded. And it's…well, just listen. *'Please forgive me if giving a damn about the environment may inconvenience others. Yes, I have been trying to get those riverboat companies to lessen their routes for some time now. Many of them are running routes that are causing much wildlife, notably waterfowl populations, to move to new areas. And don't even get me started on the amount of litter and waste each one of those boats dumps into the Mississippi. Sorry if you don't like the way I go about these things, but get used to it because you'll see a lot more of it in the future.'*"

"Well, he does sound passionate," Camille said. "Got to give him credit for that."

As she turned down the final road that would lead them to Sully Allin, she allowed herself a momentary hope. Based on what they knew about him, Sully Allin did indeed seem to be a strong suspect—especially if the chatter on Facebook turned out to be true. It echoed what McCutcheon had told them when she'd sent them off on this case—that people in high places within the government wanted this case wrapped quickly, before it made headline news and before the public, specifically tourists, caught wind that there was anything amiss. Wrapping up this case so quickly would certainly put her in a favorable spot in her new director's eyes. It would also pretty much solidify a partnership with Palmer—an agent she was already starting to understand in a variety of ways.

The paved road came to an end. A single bump was the only transition between the cracked, paved road and the hardpacked dirt road that led to the large yard that sat at the bottom of a slight hill. What surprised Camille was the state of Sully Allin's house. It was not rundown and derelict like so many of the others they'd passed on the way here. In fact, Allin's home was quite nice. It was a standard-looking cabin hugged by a wraparound porch. A large picture window looked out onto the front yard and an impressive bit of landscaping had been done along the sides, incorporating the rough swampland greens with more traditional yard-based flowers.

Two sheds sat side-by-side on the western edge of the property and off to the back; beyond a slightly sloped backyard, a bit of marshland could be seen. As Camille parked at the end of a small gravel driveway, she speculated that the marshland likely trickled into the Mississippi at some point. It was a pretty convenient location for a man that seemed to be so interested in the care of the river and also needed access to waterways for a job he seemed to be so passionate about.

As they walked toward the house, Camille could hear the sound of an engine purring along somewhere off in the distance. Maybe a lawnmower a few properties over, or a boat out in the marsh. The exact moment she looked in the direction of the sound, another sound interrupted the otherwise quiet of the day.

It was loud and unmistakable. Gunshots. Two of them, loud booming ones that sounded like reports from a shotgun.

And then a scream, followed by another shot.

Camille and Palmer shared a quick, tense look as they both drew their Glocks.

"That came from the river, right?" she asked.

"Yeah, and it was damned close."

That was all the confirmation she needed. Glock in hand and her eyes to the marshland behind the house, Camille started forward and suddenly, gators weren't the only deadly thing she was worried about.

CHAPTER FIFTEEN

Camille hurried around the side of the house, using it as a cover in the event the shooter was within sight of the property. As she and Palmer moved towards the back yard, another shout came. It was hard to tell if it was one of agony or alarm. Either way, she supposed, it was someone in need of help.

They came to the back of the house and she peered out quickly. She couldn't see anyone, but she could still hear the engine further off. Out past the back yard, there was an old, rickety dock. Two boats were tied to it—a standard aluminum fishing boat and a badly maintained johnboat with an outboard motor jutting off the back.

"You know how to drive one of those?" Camille asked.

"I know enough," he said. "You?"

"Same as you. If we—"

Another gunshot sounded out. This time, being so exposed and out in the open, they both froze and went to the ground. Still not seeing the shooter, it made Camille feel silly. And as the shot echoed, she was quite sure the shooter was on the other side of a thick, mostly-dead grove of trees on the right edge of the marsh.

"What the hell is going on over there?" Palmer yelled.

Camille, of course, had no answer. Staying low in a crouch, she rushed over to the dock. It was quite sturdy, despite looking as if it a strong wind might blow it over. She kept her eyes ahead of her, scanning the immediate area. Palmer took this cue as her laying down cover for him and made his way into the old johnboat. As he did, Camille thought she could see the slightest bit of movement through the criss-crossing of trees ahead of her, a bit further out into the marshes.

"Well," Palmer said quietly. "There's no need for keys for this thing. The engine's a pull-crank. Must be one of Allin's. Hopefully he won't mind if we take it."

Camille quickly turned to the boat and stepped in. It wobbled underneath her as she immediately turned back to face the marsh. She prepared herself as Palmer started working at the motor. It took three pulls for him to get the little outboard motor going. He then untied the boat from the dock and pushed them off. The engine puttered and coughed, almost stalling out.

"This thing is a hunk of junk," Palmer said. He turned the wheel, pointing them in the direction of the gunshots.

Camille did her best to center herself, realizing that they may very well be riding a very shaky boat into a gunfight situation. She was a good shot and had plenty of real-time experience outside of firing ranges and courses, but the prospect of having to fire her weapon at a human being was never something she relished.

The trees loomed ahead, growing closer. As Palmer guided the boat to the left to cut around them, another boat came into view right away. It was a larger boat and looked to have been taken care of. It wasn't a fancy speedboat by any means—they were, after all, out on the swamp—but it was worlds better than the deathtrap she and Palmer were currently in.

Perhaps because of the ugly sound of their motor, the two men in the larger boat had clearly heard them. One was a very large man, though the baggy clothes he was wearing made it hard to tell if he was overweight or muscular. The other was a middle-aged man wearing overalls and a dirty hat on his head. He was holding a shotgun, the barrel pointed to the water.

That's when Camille saw the large object on the back—well, hanging half-in the boat. The large man had apparently been lugging it into the boat. It was an alligator. Still and motionless, it was quite clearly dead. And suddenly, the gunshots made a lot more sense. The two men were speaking to one another, but it went unheard over the puttering of the small boat's motor.

Sensing this, Palmer killed the motor before Camille even asked. The two boats were roughly fifty feet apart with just some floating debris between them. Thin, towering trees hugged in close on the left and were almost mirrored perfectly on the right. Behind the nicer boat, it all seemed to merge into one thick, black net.

"Are either of you gentlemen Sully Allin?" Camille asked. She'd lowered her gun but it was still out. She made a point to hold it so that the men could see it.

"Yeah, that's me," said the older man in overalls. "And let me ask…who the hell are you? You're on my boat, you know. If you're trying to steal it, you're doing a shit job."

"We heard gunshots," Palmer said. "We came out to see what was going on."

“We’re with the FBI,” Camille said. “We were hoping to ask you some questions.”

The large man looked down at the alligator body, as if guilty. But Sully Allin didn’t seem to be bothered by their presence at all. “You want to ask *me* some questions after you just helped yourself to my boat? What kind of crap is that?”

“Sir, we told you—,” Camille started.

But Allin wasn’t having it. He set his shotgun down and plopped himself down behind the wheel of the boat. It was such a brazen thing to do that Camille didn’t fully understand what he was doing until he started the engine. At the same time, the large man hauled the rest of the alligator in, yanking hard to pull the massive body along the back of the boat.

“Mr. Allin!” Camille yelled.

But he was already turning the boat away from them, pointing it deeper into the marshlands.

“Damn,” Palmer said, starting to pull at the crank on the motor again. As it missed on his first, second, and third tries, Camille had to watch helplessly as Allin, his counterpart, and the dead gator escaped. The boat was fast, but was slightly bogged down by the weight of the gator on the back.

The fourth tug at the pull crank got the motor going again. “That’s right,” Palmer said. “We’re about to have a medium-speed chase on a piece of shit fishing boat in a swamp.” He sounded irritated but there was something akin to a childlike delight in his voice.

He gunned the motor and the boat lurched, almost stalling out again. Palmer let out a curse, tried again without so much speed, and the boat surged forward.

“You think he’s running because we caught him killing a gator?” Camille yelled over the motor.

“It’s not against the law to kill a gator on public land. You’d think a man that quote-unquote rescues them would know that sort of thing. No…I think there’s something else going on here.”

Camille thought so, too. She positioned herself at the front of the boat with her Glock still drawn and her eyes set ahead. As Palmer brought the boat whipping around a downed, floating stump, she saw Allin’s boat much farther ahead. Allin was still facing forward, but the larger man was facing them. He called out something over his shoulder.

She knew she had no right to shoot at them. Not in this situation. But she also knew that even with the gator on the back of their boat, they were going to likely outpace them if it did come down to a race on these swampy waters. She was starting to fully understand why Allin had left this little boat behind. Not only would the weight of a dead gator sink the damned thing, but the motor was nearing the end of its life.

"You up for this?" Camille called back to Palmer. "Maybe I should call it in and have someone try to cut them off."

"We could…but do you have any idea where he's headed?"

"Good point," she said.

Behind her, she heard and felt Palmer take the risk of giving the little motor a bit more gas. It sputtered just a bit but then smoothed out. The boat sped along, Palmer swerving a bit to avoid hitting a large branch from a fallen tree. And as the boat ahead of them grew smaller and started to slowly veer off to the left behind a thicket of weeds and saplings, she worried that they were going to lose the first real lead of this case.

CHAPTER SIXTEEN

In terms of a chase, Camille thought it felt almost boring. Neither of the boats had much power—theirs because of its age and lack of maintenance and Allin's because of the added weight of the gator on the back. Still, there was the anticipation of how it would all end, of how it would play out. She kept reminding herself that there was at least one gun on the boat ahead of them, a large rifle that had been used to apparently kill a gator.

"I don't get why the asshole would run," Palmer called from the wheel.

"I'm guessing reputation," Camille said. "His website and Facebook pages portray him as this gentle, kind man that takes care to move these animals safely. And we just caught him slaughtering one."

"Well, this medium-speed chase through the swamps isn't going to help him any."

Camille kept her eyes ahead. Allin's boat had gone around a bank and was out of sight, but she could still see the small crests and disturbance in the water where he had passed. She figured as long as she could still see details like these, she'd be able to keep track of their location, namely if they decided to hit a bank and escape on foot through the woods.

As she scanned the water, she also kept an eye out for other gators. She recalled all of the stories she'd grown up around—of how they were menacing and cunning. And the fact that she'd come face-to-face with them not once but *two* times during her last case was still sitting heavy in her mind.

It took only another minute or so of tearing through the stagnant water before even the signs of Allin's boat ahead of them came to a stop. They were far enough away now that the water was still. She wanted to signal for Palmer to kill the engine so she could listen for signs of the other boat ahead but knew that losing those seconds could be detrimental to the chase. Instead, she kept her eyes toward the banks, looking for any sign that they may have moored the boat and taken off.

Gaunt trees and tall weeds hugged the banks, cattails sticking up out of the water like bizarre road signs. She realized that for someone that knew the lay of the land well, there were infinite hiding spots. And if Allin and his large friend got too far ahead of them, they'd be gone for good. There could be a manhunt, sure, but she really hoped it wouldn't come to that—especially given McCutcheon's plea to wrap this case up as soon as possible. A manhunt for a potential suspect wasn't going to help matters at all on that end of things.

As Palmer brought the boat around a slight leftward bend in the river, Camille took note of three birds taking off on her right. They went fluttering up from a thick group of tall weeds, yellowed and dried in the sun. Camille studied the weeds and saw a very gradual indentation near the center of the cluster. And among the tall, brittle grass, she spotted the briefest speck of blue…the same denim shade as the overalls Allin's friend was wearing.

Killing the engine and trying to convince them to come out of hiding seemed foolish. Keeping the engine going and trying to fool them, however, might work well. She had an idea, though it was a bit reckless, especially when she kept in mind there was a rifle on board Allin's boat.

Camille turned back to Palmer and subtly nodded over to the weeds. Then, keeping her hands low (the Glock still held in her right), she made a slow, slight motion of both hands striking one another.

Palmer looked hesitant at first but finally nodded as a slight smirk came across his face. He shrugged, eyed the cluster of tall weeds and gradually started steering the boat in that direction. The water seemed to hum beneath the little boat as they drew closer to the weeds—then closer and closer.

At the last moment, as the boat was roughly ten feet away from the weeds, Palmer gave the little motor a bit more gas. As it lurched forward, Camille got down to her knee in the best shooter's stance she could manage on a moving boat. She also stiffened her ankles and leaned back slightly against the small barrier that separated the front of the boat from the driver's chair, bracing for the impact.

When the boat tore through the weeds, the sound of it being crushed was like paper being crumpled. Camille only heard it for a moment, though; their boat collided with Allin's a mere second after it came into view, positioned strategically just off center of the clump of weeds.

The impact wasn't quite as fierce as she'd expected and that was perhaps the most surprising thing of all. This was apparently not the case for Allin and his large friend, though. When Camille's eyes were able to focus on the commotion on his boat, she saw Sully fighting for balance. As for the large man in overalls, he was already trying to leap out of the back of the boat—*trying* being the operative word. As he tried to make his escape, his left leg got caught on the alligator corpse. Rather than leaping from the boat, he toppled over, banging the side of his head on the back of the boat. In any other situation, it may have been funny…even though the gator did make it a bit frightening.

Camille got to her feet and stepped to the edge of their boat. Before she made the stride across the sides of the two boats, Sully Allin made the slightest of moves towards the rifle, which had been knocked to the floor in the small crash.

"That would be a very stupid decision," Camille said, leveling her Glock at him. "Make it easier on all of us and just forget it's there."

"What in the hell do you want with me anyway?" Allin asked in a near-hiss. he was scared, sure, but there was an arrogant defiance in his voice and his posture. As far as he was concerned, he was being unjustly attacked.

"Well, at first it was just to ask you a few questions," Palmer said, joining in beside Camille. "Now, given the little swamp chase you just led us on, I think we have a few more things to discuss."

"Is it because of *that?"* he asked, pointing back to the alligator on the back of the boat. In doing so, he saw for the first time what had happened to his friend. He looked disgusted and when he turned his eyes back to Camille and Palmer, Camille could see that he was only now starting to understand the sort of trouble he had potentially gotten into. And the dead gator strung along the back of the boat was a very large piece of evidence indeed.

"No, not quite," Camille asked. She then stepped over into his boat, her Glock still out but no longer trained on him as she stepped into the space between Allin and the rifle.

"Hands behind your back, Mr. Allin," Palmer said as he, too, stepped over onto the other boat.

"This is messed up," Allin said, but he did as Palmer asked. "You steal *my* boat and then *ram me with it* and somehow, I'm the one that's under arrest."

"We can sort all of that out at the station," Camille said. "And we'll also see about getting your friend some medical attention."

The large man was doing his best to get to his feet but had apparently knocked himself silly. He was currently holding himself up and leaning against the edge of the boat, nearly falling over into the water.

Camille made a point to remain in front of the rifle just in case the big man was faking it. But the trickle of blood along the side of his head suggested he was not. She watched as Palmer pulled Allin's arms behind his back and cuffed him. Camille did the same to the large man, finding that his dizziness was not an act at all. He was so dizzy that both of them nearly spilled into the water as she slapped the handcuffs around his wrists. It took an immense amount of strength to keep him upright long enough to position him in a steady posture. She sat him gently down into the seat and then, with Palmer's help, pushed the dead gator into the shallow water. It was brutally heavy and for a moment, she didn't think they'd be able to move it. After some hard work and pushing, it moved down into the water in an anti-climactic splash.

"Well that's just a waste!" Allin said.

"I'm sure it appreciates your concern," Palmer said.

With the gator in its final resting place and both men cuffed, Palmer got behind the wheel and clumsily backed the boat away from the now-ruined smaller boat. He then guided it out of the weeds with an oar before pointing it back down the river, retracing the water in the direction they had come, now with two handcuffed men in their company.

CHAPTER SEVENTEEN

Escorting Sully Allin through the rear entrance of the field office headquarters was a vastly different experience than the last time she'd hauled a gator handler into an interrogation room. Rather than marching him through an accommodating and often busy precinct lobby, she and Palmer moved him through the quiet, brightly lit halls of the field office. Under the fluorescent lights, Allin's sun-burned skin appeared almost lobster-red. She wondered, though, how much of the red in his face had come from embarrassment and anger.

She was just glad they hadn't been tasked with getting his very large friend inside. That had been undertaken by two much sturdier agents, taking him to another room.

As Camille sat him down in one of their polished and clean interrogation rooms, Palmer took a moment to log the event into the system and make sure all cameras were working. When he came back in, he had a bottle of water, which he handed over to Allin.

"Why am I in an FBI office?" Allin asked.

"Because we're FBI agents, on a case assigned to us by the FBI," Palmer said.

"The FBI is interested in gator poaching?"

"Not so much," Palmer said. "We're not interested in you and your gator-related business, though it *may* come up later down the road."

"Or now," Camille said. "Your site says you treat them humanely. So what did we happen to witness today?"

"A side business that I'd very much like to keep under wraps," Allin said.

"Poaching alligators?" Camille asked.

"More or less," he said. He seemed to be a little more willing to talk now, assured they weren't interested in that part of his life. "I have a guy down in Florida that pays me for gator hides. He manufactures and sells wallets, shoes, handbags, that sort of thing. But…well, you said that's not why you came after me."

"That's right," Camille said. "But on the other hand, you do know that it's illegal to not only poach gators but to then sell any products made from their hides. Right?"

"Yes. But—"

"Mr. Allin, do you spend a lot of time on riverboats?" Camille asked.

The question seemed to confuse him, so sudden and out of the blue. "Like…you mean *riding* on them?"

"Yes."

"No, I don't. I can't remember the last time I was on a riverboat. Maybe two years ago. One of those little casino-style ones. I remember it because I had a bit too much to drink but I did come off of there about three hundred dollars richer."

"You're sure about that?"

"Yes…well, maybe not the exact timing. I'm pretty sure it was early fall, though."

"But you claim to have not been on a riverboat in the past year, correct?"

"That's right."

Camille knew what she wanted to ask next and she also already had a feeling as to how it was going to go. She could feel Allin slipping away moment by moment. She kept thinking of the dead alligator on the back of his boat—specifically how much time, effort, and planning may have gone into it.

"If we were to ask you for your whereabouts this morning as well as a few different times over the past week, could you provide alibis?"

"Depends on when during the week. As for this morning, yeah, I can, though. Me and Dwayne—that's the other guy you cuffed after he whacked his head when you crashed into us—met for breakfast at this little diner called Muddy Mo's. Talked about heading out and catching at least one gator today. After that, we headed back to my house, got all the equipment ready and set out. We'd been on the water for about two and a half hours by the time you showed up."

"Did anyone see you at this diner?" Palmer asked.

"Yeah. I spoke to at least four other people. Two of them at length."

"Could you provide their names and numbers if asked."

"Yeah. And they'd vouch for me, too." He eyed them both with anger and suspicion, the redness in his face growing a bit. "You crashed my boats and dragged me in here, swearing it has nothing to do with the gators. So what the hell is really going on?"

Camille and Palmer exchanged a look, measuring one another up. It was becoming clearer and clearer that he might not be their guy after all, especially given that he had what seemed like an easy-to-prove alibi for at least one of the murders. They didn't *need* to tell him the specifics of the case but they did, by law, have to at least give him an indication of why they had come after him.

"We're dealing with a series of murders, all of which have taken place over the course of the past four days," Palmer said. "The most recent occurred this morning. Right now, we have reason to believe our person of interest may have had a passion for environmental conservation. And according to the copy on your website, you lined up with that. Of course, after witnessing you and your buddy out there with that alligator, I'm assuming your website is a bit misleading."

"You mean to tell me I'm here on suspicion of murder?"

"Yes, you lined up with the sort of suspect we were looking for," Camille said. "And your poaching of that alligator and the fact you tried running from us only increased our suspicions, especially given the rosy picture your website paints of you. It doesn't really line up with what we saw today. But if your alibis do indeed line up, you'll be free to go. What happens in terms of what you've been doing to those gators is more of a game warden issue, so we won't have control over that."

Allin looked to the table, thinking all of this over. He shook his head and said, "I can tell you right now that I've never killed anyone."

Camille believed him. She believed him enough to move on to their next step while other agents looked in on his alibis. It would take some phone calls to get it done but she was sure McCutcheon would be fine with that use of additional resources if she wanted this case closed as soon as possible. Just knowing this was a bit of a relief because it meant she and Palmer could continue to sniff out leads while other agents made calls and interviews to knock out alibis.

Camille stepped back towards the door, her hand on the knob. "We'll look into those alibis. Anything else you want to add?"

He only shook his head, still looking as if he were trying to decide if he should be angry or frightened of the possible outcome of all of this. Camille walked out of the room and Palmer followed, closing the door behind him.

"His alibi for this morning sounds like an easy one to prove," Palmer said.

"Yeah, it does. If he gets in any sort of trouble, it's only going to be for gator poaching." What she thought, but didn't say out loud out of fear of seeming defeated, was: *He was a total waste of our time.*

"So where do we go from here?" Palmer asked. "The day is getting late and if this thing rolls into another day or, God help us, another victim, I think McCutcheon might go nuclear."

Camille, having never seen the bad side of her new director, had no interest in seeing such a thing. She started to think about the tickets the victims needed to get on the riverboat. She thought of the routes the riverboats had taken and how they might line up. It was more sitting and studying, but it was the only thing she could think of. It seemed that this entire case might very well come down to the riverboats.

"I want to see maps of the routes these riverboats take. I want departure times, docking times, everything."

"That's a lot of phone calls," Palmer said in a discouraging tone.

"I know," Camille said. "So we'd better get started."

CHAPTER EIGHTEEN

Dusk settled across the river like a quilt, bringing with it cooler temperatures and the start of the night songs of crickets and frogs. Terry Winsome sat in her unremarkable little aluminum boat and watched the sunlight dim across the water. Though she was one of forty participants in the Caterwaul Bass Tournament, she was alone on the river. In fact, she wasn't *quite* on the river. She'd elected to use a little waterway that came off the Mississippi, one of the little streams that could almost be considered nothing more than a creek.

Terry had discovered this little spot about three years ago when she'd come out with her husband. Over beers and cheese crackers, they'd pulled bass after bass out of this little spot, tucked away behind tangles of water-logged trees, weeds, and an assortment of swamp-like plants. And it was a spot that never disappointed. She *had* found, though, that she had to be careful when coming out here as there were at least twenty different forks off this little stream. Some led to dead-ends of crabgrass and fallen trees while others led to swampy regions.

She'd caught four bass already, but none had been that special one that was going to win her the tournament. The last one she'd caught had been damn near twenty-five pounds and she'd tossed it back. Twenty-five pounds wasn't going to win her the tournament. And God knew she could use the ten grand that came with first place.

She cast her line back out, thinking of her husband—*missing* her husband. He'd died in a car accident just seven months ago. This was the first tournament she'd participated in since his passing and she thought it would be fitting to win it for him…well, him and the large cash prize.

She checked her watch and saw that she had to be back at the tournament grounds in an hour and a half. That would give her another twenty minutes to fish, leaving her plenty of time to get the aluminum boat back to her speedboat, which she'd left docked back about half a mile behind her because it would not fit in the folds and turns of her secret spot. She had plenty of time *and* she knew that dusk was a very good time to fish. She did, however, start to regret tossing that twenty-pounder back.

As she watched her line in the black water, she heard a small sound behind her. Something stirring in the water. Maybe a snake or a lost duck. She turned to see what was making the noise and was surprised to see a boat much like her own coming through the thin stream.

Is this another fisherman? she wondered. *Who else could possibly know about this spot? It's in the middle of absolutely nowhere.*

Just as she was about to wonder if someone had been sneaky and followed her, she saw the man rowing the boat. She was pretty sure he wasn't one of the other fishermen she was competing against. While he *did* have a rod and reel in the boat, it was a cheap one—the sort you could get for about fifty bucks at any Wal-Mart.

She gave him a nod, assuming he was just some hobbyist out to explore the outer ridges of the river. He nodded back as the rest of his tiny boat came into view around a cluster of weeds and thin saplings that had nearly been drowned out by the river. And as he returned that gesture, Terry realized that she knew him. Well, maybe not *knew* him, but she'd certainly seen him before.

Ah Jesus, she thought. *This guy...*

He had a small piece of land on the other side of the grove she was currently floating next to. He'd caught her on his bank once before, and then floating by it another time. Both times, he'd been something of an ass about it, claiming that she was polluting the rivers and trespassing on his land. But now, with her line in the water, she was at least a quarter of a mile away from his property. She'd made sure of it when she'd tossed her anchor out.

"I'm nowhere near your property," she said. "I made sure of it."

"I know," the man said. He was smirking at her, and she couldn't tell if there was malice or just a very pretentious sarcasm. "Still doesn't mean I want you out here."

"This isn't *your* land," she argued, starting to get angry. "And look, I'm in the middle of a fishing tournament here and—"

Terry wasn't aware of what he was doing until it was too late. The maniac was purposefully using his oar to maneuver his boat so that it would collide with hers. Was the asshole trying to knock her out of the boat?

"What are you *doing?"* she yelled.

The boats did indeed collide. Her rod was knocked into the water and she nearly fell out herself as she leaned over to grasp it. She turned to yell at him, hell, to maybe smack him across his stupid face with her oar. As she did, she saw him place something into his mouth. A cigarette? Or maybe a straw?

She heard him make a harsh blowing noise and then there was something at her neck. It felt like a bee sting but she knew that wasn't quite right.

"What are you d—"

Her words stopped, seizing up in her throat. And as she tried to raise the oar to attack him, she realized that her arms were no longer working, either. She felt almost paralyzed and there was something like an itch at the back of her throat. She reached up to massage her throat, looking to the man with wide, bewildered eyes.

His expression tuned into a smile as he brought his boat alongside hers. He grabbed the edge of her boat and simply sat there, waiting.

Terry felt like she had to throw up but at the same time, could not seem to draw in a breath. She tried screaming, tried reaching for her phone, but nothing worked. Her body was shutting down and the world seemed to be going a dark shade of purple.

And all the while, that man sat in his boat, smiling. Waiting.

In the end, Terry managed to look away from him. The purple turned to black and she'd be damned if that smiling evil face was the last thing she saw. In that regard, she was fortunate. And as the black closed in and the need to breathe became paralyzing, she could only hope that her husband would be somewhere beyond that blackness, waiting for her on the other side.

CHAPTER NINETEEN

There was too much going on with the case to confine everything to Camille's office. Instead, she and Palmer moved into one of several conference rooms within in the field office headquarters. With the help of a few other agents and interns, they'd gotten everything they needed within forty minutes: maps of the routes the *Whistlin' Pig* and *Wheeler's Delight* had taken on the days of the murders, a schedule of all departure and docking times, and even a list of all employees that had been on board each boat on the days of the murders.

Camille had taped the maps to a large dry erase board, each route traced out in highlighter with the times jotted down in marker beneath them. On the other side of the board she'd jotted down facts of the case they believed could hold true. A new one occurred to her as she compared the routes of each boat.

She turned her head just to make sure Palmer was still sitting at the conference table. He'd been running in and out of the room for the past fifteen minutes or so while also looking over the records of the boats' employees. He was at the computer again, scanning the screen with great concentration.

"Being that the boats are owned by two different companies, I think it's safe to rule out the owners or anyone investing in either company," she said. "So as far as I'm concerned, that rules out the murders being done as some sort of competitive retribution."

"Agreed. And so far, I'm pretty sure we can eliminate at least six of the seven employees I've looked into. And quite frankly, I'm not sure what that leaves us. Aside from waiting and hoping that something comes back from forensics or the coroner's reports...what can we do?"

It was a good question. And even though she hated to feel as if she was wasting time with the maps and the voyage times, Camille had to feel as if she were doing *something.* She compared the times to see if there were similarities, but the times of departure and docking for each trip were just as varied as the type of victims. The same was true of the sites and landmarks each trip had passed by. It started to become infuriating to know that the deeper they dug into the details of this case, the *less* it seemed that the victims or the boats were linked in any particular way.

"What about the cities?" she asked out loud, for no reason other than hoping Palmer could maybe springboard off one of her flimsy theories. "There are a few points of interest each of the trips passed by. They all stay within New Orleans proper, but the trips that Brittany Gable and Kevin Pleasant were on *did* travel a bit outside of what most people would consider the city limits."

After a few moments of silence, she turned to look at him again. He was reclining back in his chair with his arms crossed against his chest. "I think that's…well, to be honest, I think that's a stretch. The times of day are different, not to mention the boats themselves."

"I know, it's just—"

A knock at the door interrupted her, and both she and Palmer turned to see the door open up. Camille was expecting it to be another of the interns, perhaps with more information about the boat schedules or background checks on all known employees and even the list of passengers Palmer had started to compile—which was a small list indeed, as getting credit card information for that many people was a task in and of itself.

But the figure at the door was no intern. It was AD McCutcheon, standing in the doorway and looking stone-faced.

"Agents," she said.

Neither Camille nor Palmer said anything. McCutcheon's face said it all. And then, just to seal the deal, so did her lips: "There's been another murder."

***

It was dark when they stepped out into the parking lot and the night somehow seemed to grow even darker as they neared the river. It didn't help that the new body had been discovered adrift in a little aluminum boat roughly three miles away from any sort of illuminated building or sign of any kind. In fact, they had to take a series of little back roads to get to the boat landing the police had moved the boat to.

The boat ramp had been blocked off with crime scene tape, so fresh that the man holding the spool of tape was walking away from one of the posts he'd used to put it up when they arrived. Camille and Palmer walked down the ramp where three cops were huddled around a cheap aluminum fishing boat. Even the disaster of a boat they'd used to chase down Sully Allin had been a more reliable looking boat than this one.

The woman inside looked to be in her forties. There were two expensive fishing rods and a tacklebox stowed away in the boat as well. Even in the glaring mobile lights the police had set up, Camille could tell the death was recent; it showed in the pallor of the skin and even the semi-brightness of the woman's opened eyes.

Seeing it set off a spark off in Camille's heart. This killer was moving fast and there was no telling what he might be capable of before they were able to catch him. How many more bodies would there be?

It unnerved her, but she tucked the worry away for now, trying to focus on the here and now.

"How far away was the boat when it was discovered?" Palmer asked.

The cop standing in the center of the trio of officers answered: "About half a mile to the west. Just sort of floating around aimlessly. Ironically, the man that found it was part of a fishing tournament that was taking place today. And this woman was also a participant."

"So we already have an ID on her?" Camille asked.

"Terry Winsome, forty-one years of age. There was an abandoned speedboat anchored along a bank about half a mile away, too. We're waiting for records to come back on it, but we think it belonged to her, as well. There was paperwork for the tournament with her name on it found inside."

Camille dropped to her knees and peered inside the boat. The fact that it was a dead body that had been found on the river made her want to instantly connect it to their killer—a killer that seemed to be ramping things up considerably. But then again, the others had been found in the water, having been tossed from riverboats. So this new body didn't seem to fit quite as easily.

"You said the boat was just drifting in the water?" Camille asked.

"That's what the fisherman that found her said. He's right up at the top of the ramp, in the parking lot, if you want to talk to him."

"Yeah, I think we might do that."

But before she walked away from the body, Camille used a Maglite to get a better look at the victim. There seemed to be some slight discoloration around the throat, similar to what they'd seen with Brittany Gable. Just as she was about to look away, she saw something else. At first, she thought it was just a fleck of dirt or grime but as she leaned in, she realized it was something else entirely.

"Who's got gloves on?" she asked loudly.

There was some movement behind her as a cop stepped forward. "I'm wearing some. Why? What do you need?"

"See that spot high up on her neck, just before the jaw?"

The cop leaned down, nearly kneeling now himself. "Yeah, I see it."

"Try moving it. See if it's dirt or something."

He did, but the mark remained there. It was small, no larger than a pin prick, really, but the area around it was irritated enough to make it stand out.

"Hey, Palmer…what does this look like to you?" She knew what *she* thought it was but wanted to hear another voice of reason before making a call on it.

She sensed him stepping behind her to get a look. "I want to say an injection of some kind, but that's a very strange place for an injection. Maybe it's a bug bite of some kind?"

The cop that had investigated the odd wound felt around it again and shook his head. "I don't feel where it's raised or inflamed."

"Then an injection site," Camille said, getting to her feet. "And based on the redness around it, I'd say it's very recent, too. Officers, can you point me to the fisherman that found the body?"

Two men directed her further up the ramp, where a partially paved parking lot fed out into a connector road. That road wound off into the dark distance, back to the secondary road she and Palmer had taken to get out here. They walked up and found a man standing by the side of a truck. The truck had a trailer on the back, which was carrying a fishing boat. A uniformed officer was speaking to him, taking notes.

"Excuse us, officer," Camille said, showing her badge. "Agents Grace and Palmer, with the FBI. Can we have a word with him?"

The officer closed the notebook he was using to take notes and gave them a polite nod as he walked away, back down the ramp to the body.

"FBI, huh?" the man asked. He was slightly overweight, wearing a basic tee shirt and cargo shorts. A visor rested on his head, covering half of his unruly black hair. "That was quick. I guess news travels fast."

"We have suspicions that this death could potentially be linked to others that have occurred recently," Palmer said. "Sir, what's your name?"

"Greg Maxwell."

"Mr. Maxwell, are you familiar with the area of the river where you found the body?" Camille asked.

"A bit. I was moving over there because I wasn't having luck at my usual spots."

"On your way to this side of the river, did you pass lots of other boats?"

"A few. But that's to be expected because of the tournament. There were forty folks in it this time around."

"I'm curious," Palmer said. "How many are you allowed to take out of the river for this tournament?"

"Just one. You hope to land a big one and take your chances, hoping no one else can beat that *one* when you call it a day. The rest of it is catch and release."

"And what about the victim? Terry Winsome. Did you know her?"

"Not personally, but I knew *of* her. She used to participate in these tournaments all the time. Her husband died not too long ago and she sort of took a break. I think this was her first one back since he passed away."

"Any chance you know where she may have been headed or coming from when you came across her boat?"

"No clue. And to be honest, it's a freak accident that I saw her out there at all. I was about to turn around and head back. But then I saw her in that boat…which I thought was weird."

"Why is that?"

"It was just a little aluminum boat, that thing she's in. When she started earlier today, she was in the speedboat the cops are looking into right now."

"So she switched boats at some point?" Camille asked.

"I guess so. Some people do it pretty often. You take a faster boat to some of those little sidewinding streams that taper off of the river. You get some good bass and trout, maybe a few catfish here and there in places like that. But to me, it's a waste of time. You spend more time fighting your way through weeds and brush than you do fishing."

"So based on the boat you found her in, do you think it's a safe bet that's what she was doing?"

"Yeah," Maxwell said. "I think it's pretty likely. I told the cops the same thing and they're supposedly getting a team together to go out there and look around those little outlets and streams. But in the middle of the night…shit. Good luck with that."

"And you're sure she was dead when you found her?"

"Pretty sure. She wasn't responding…not blinking, either."

Camille looked back down to the bottom of the ramp where the officers were still huddled around the boat that contained the body of Terry Winsome. If this *was* related, there was no way the killer could have a big head-start on them. But it was also clear that the killer knew the river and the off-shoots that fed out into countless swampy and depleted regions.

As her mind tried to pin down one particular area to focus on, Scott wrapped up the discussion with Maxwell. "Thanks for your time. Here's my business card. If you think of anything else or hear anything from the other tournament participants, please give me a call."

They left Greg Maxwell to the cop that had been questioning him and made their way back down to the little aluminum boat. One of the cops hurried over to them, a cellphone in his hand.

"I just got word that they're sending four or five boats out to check some of the sidewinding little streams that Mrs. Winsome could have come from. Want me to see if they've got room on those boats for you two?"

"I don't know," Camille said. Secretly, today's little boat excursion in chasing down Sully Allin had soured her on the idea of getting on another boat anytime soon. Also, it seemed like a good way to get stranded out on the water if something else in the case *did* break.

Palmer seemed to read her mind. "Thanks, but I think we're good. There's more we can do on land."

"For starters, I want a request for a tox screen done on her body." Then, looking to Palmer, she added: "And we should look into that with the other three bodies, just in case."

In saying that, Camille understood that sometime between finding the injection site on the neck and turning down an offer to explore the creeks and streams at night, she'd decided that this likely *was* the work of their killer. And in making that call, she had to face the fact that this man was moving fast and was somehow already several steps ahead of them with his latest victim not yet even cold.

CHAPTER TWENTY

Camille was exhausted but as she looked over the reports the coroner had sent over, she wondered if this might be the first night as an agent in New Orleans that she ended up sleeping in her office. She and Palmer once again found themselves in her basement space, a pizza on the small table between her desk and the little loveseat.

"So here's another thing to consider," Palmer said, pulling her attention away from the tox screens of Brittany Gable and Kevin Pleasant; it would be at least another hour or so before she got Natania Whitehead's results and maybe as many as six before they saw Terry Winsome's. "Greg Maxwell said the tournament was catch and release style. It wasn't like the participants were stockpiling their catches."

"Okay," Camille said. "Why does that matter?"

"Because if we're still operating on the assumption that the killer is somehow trying to take out people that seem to be harming the rivers and surrounding areas, you'd think the idea of catch-and-release would be welcome to someone with that mindset."

"Unless it's just the act of fishing itself that angers him," Camille pointed out. "And here's something else that's bothering me. If the killer did indeed attack her while she was in one of those little cut-away areas off the river, he would have had to have *known* she'd be there."

"Or followed her."

"Or that," she conceded. "And if we want to explore that route, I think we need to look into everyone that was in that tournament."

"Call it a gut hunch sort of thing," Palmer said, "but I feel like it's not that. If we're assuming Winsome is indeed the fourth victim of our killer, that means our killer has been busy. I doubt that left him time to enter a tournament. Besides…he killed Natania Whitehead this morning. And according to what I saw on the tournament Facebook page, start time was very early this morning."

Camille nodded, turning her attention back to her laptop and the PDFs of the tox screens they currently had. They were preliminary and showed only the surface level results, though. For anything deeper and more specific, she was going to have to wait a bit longer. And she already thought that was going to be the case because what she had in front of her showed nothing.

Okay, so maybe Winsome isn't another victim of our killer, she thought. *That injection site, right in the neck...how does that even happen?*

Then an idea came to her. It wasn't a big one, but it did seem relevant. "Hold on. Brittany Gable had been sick before she was tossed overboard. The girls at the party said so, remember?"

"Yeah, they thought it was maybe some bad crawfish or shrimp."

"What if it wasn't? What if she'd been poisoned?"

Palmer shrugged and nodded to her laptop. "What do the reports say?"

Camille sighed and said, "Nothing. Not a damned thing. But these are just preliminary results."

She could feel her mind winding down, numbing over, trying to convince her that she was tired and needed to get some shut-eye. Even if it was just a thirty-minute nap, that would be something. She knew what it felt like to keep attacking a case even when exhaustion crept in, and she knew that it often led to oversights and mistakes.

But with Palmer here with her, she couldn't allow herself such a luxury. Not that she was trying harder than necessary to create a good impression—she simply didn't want to appear unprofessional or lazy.

She supposed she could set her mind to some other task and maybe switch gears for a moment. Instantly, her mind went to Zack Hayes, the zoologist she still hadn't texted. He'd be in town soon enough and she didn't intend on blowing him off. She picked up her phone, wondering.

"Give me a second, would you?" she told Palmer as she got to her feet and exited the room.

"It's your office," he said. "You can ask me to leave."

"No big deal. I'll just be a second."

She closed the door behind her as she stepped out into the basement hallway. She took her phone from her pocket, fully intending to call Zack. It was nearing eleven o' clock so she hesitated, wondering if it might be too late to call. And then, as she considered the time, her mind drifted a bit further and she found herself thinking of Deanna. Maybe it was because of the weird link between the church Zack was going to for the memorial service and her mother's past. It was all very blurry and convoluted, but it *did* make her want to speak with Deanna. Deanna would probably understand and be able to talk her through it. And even though Deanna *had* kept secrets about Nanette from her, she was willing to accept the fact that Deanna was the only real family she had. Sure, there was her father but things were so strained there that she wasn't remotely ready to talk about her mother with him. He was, in fact, the *last* person she'd ever want to talk to about her mother.

Temporarily forgetting about Zack, she pulled up Deanna's number. She pressed Call before she could talk herself out of it, ignoring the time. The phone rang only a single time in her ear before going to voicemail. Apparently, Deanna was the sort of person that either turned her phone off when she retired to bed or had it set to silent after a certain time. She had no idea what sort of message she'd end up leaving if she allowed herself to leave one, so she hung up first.

When she headed back into her office, she saw that Palmer was on his phone. She was walking in while he was in mid conversation, but it was easy to catch up. Palmer, always thinking ahead, though, walked over to the dry erase board and scribbled down: BOAT COPS.

"Yeah, well that's understandable," Palmer was saying. "I don't blame you. Yeah. Yeah. That's great, just keep us posted if anything pops up."

He ended the call and pocketed his phone. Camille noticed that he looked just as tired as she felt. "The cops said they even got some of the guys from the Environmental Conservation police to come out in the boats with them, but they found nothing. He did note that being the dead of night, the job is so much harder than it usually is, though. They're swapping out shifts now but honestly don't think they'll find anything. There's just too many little nooks and crannies over there in all that brush and scrubland."

"Yeah, I figured as much." She signed heavily and collapsed onto the loveseat. "Terry Winsome couldn't have been dead for more than an hour before Maxwell found her body. He was close by when they pulled that boat out of the water. He *had* to be. And now we're back to having nothing…just another victim."

"Exactly," Palmer said. "And sitting here staring at numbers and times and police records that I feel certain aren't going to net anything is wasting our time and energy. I say we keep our phones nearby and get some sleep while we can." He closed up his laptop and picked it up from the little table by the loveseat. "Sound like a plan?"

"Sure. Wait, Palmer…how far from here do you live?"

"Far too close. Less than ten minutes. Where's your place?"

"About twenty minutes away. I'm just going to crash here. I'd invite you, but there's no room."

"Partners shouldn't do sleepovers anyway," he said with a wink.

"Get some shut-eye, Grace. See you soon."

"Hopefully very soon," she said. "If we don't get a break on this soon..."

"I know."

He gave her a playful wave and left the office. Camille got up, shut the lights off, and returned to the loveseat. She had to stretch her legs over the armrests and let them dangle, but it was surprisingly comfortable. Her mind wandered instantly back to the river, the water flowing along under a night sky, carrying countless secrets with it. Somewhere out there, maybe even along its banks, the killer was lurking, waiting, maybe even hunting his next victim.

The river imagery faded and Camille became aware that she was drifting off. She could also sense that it was a fleeting sort of nap, the kind that would refresh her just enough to keep her going but make her crash that much harder when she was finally able to get some proper sleep. She enjoyed this sort of rest on occasion, as she could *feel* her body relaxing rather than just anchoring itself down for sleep.

It was a rest, though, that was still just barely deep enough to allow her mind to conjure up dreams and nightmares. One came to her then, in her dark office, a fragmented collage of images. She saw Nanette, her sister, floating down the Mississippi River. The water was dark but she could still see Nanette's blood trailing out behind her, creating its own current. Her sister's eyes spotted her, lounging on a bank with a fishing rod perched between her legs.

Nanette smiled, went under the water, and disappeared. And then Camille's fishing rod began to bend, as if she'd caught a massive fish. But in the nightmare, she knew it was Nanette on the other end of the line. And the question that seemed to envelop the dream was if Nanette was pulling on the line in an effort to make it to shore and save herself or if she was trying to pull Camille into the river with her.

Camille came awake with a jump, her heart in her throat and, for just a moment, her legs starting to kick as if she was fully expecting to wake up in the river. As she sat up on the loveseat, she realized that her phone was ringing. She grabbed for it on the table in front of her without even setting eyes on it. She took a moment to recalibrate herself, noting on the phone's screen that it was 3:41. She'd nearly slept for three whole hours.

She didn't recognize the number but it started with a New Orleans area code. Hoping the call would result in a break on the case, she answered: "This is Agent Grace."

"Agent Grace, this is Samuel Bourn, the coroner. I thought you'd want to know that we got the results back from the broader battery for the tox screen. There's definitely something here that you need to know about."

"What is it?"

"There's a neurotoxic peptide present in these results. It's not a particularly high dosage, but, well, these peptides can be quite lethal."

"Do you have any idea where it came from?" she asked. Camille knew a good deal about zoology, having taken it as a minor in college and never really doing much with it. She did know that certain neurotoxic peptides caused shortness of breath and vomiting. *Vomiting...just like Brittany Gable, she thought.*

There were a few others that could be fatal but for that to happen…well, it didn't make a lot of sense.

"I think I might, but it's peculiar. This certain peptide is known as a conotoxin. It comes almost exclusively from—"

"From cone snails," Camille said. "Did you find this in both Gable and Pleasant?"

"I did. It was a bit more prominent in Brittany Gable. I take it…you know a good deal about cone snails?"

"Not much. Just passing knowledge." This was true. While she'd always been interested in animals capable of producing and emitting toxins, it was not an area she was well-versed in. "There were no marks on the bodies to suggest they had been stung by cone snails, though, correct?"

"That's correct. And besides that, the amounts found in them was a bit higher than I'd expect to see from a cone snail sting."

Right away, Camille thought of the small mark in Terry Winsome's neck—a mark they'd been thinking of as an injection mark of some kind.

"Mr. Bourn, do you have any idea if people actually harvest cone snails to extract conotoxins?"

"Oh, absolutely. There's a pain killer called ziconotide that is widely used. And if I'm not mistaken, I believe there are some researchers that are experimenting with cone snail toxins in epilepsy and Alzheimer's research."

"Thank you, Mr. Bourn. Could you please email copies of those results to me?"

She ended the call, her thoughts instantly going in the direction of looking into researchers that might be using cone snails. But something about that didn't fit. In fact, when she plugged cone snails into the equation they already had—of a man that seemed bent on preserving his home turf by any means necessary—she became more confident that they were on the right track. This was a man that knew the area intimately. She knew that cone snails did live around the area, mostly in shallow waters along the river and under coral shelves along the coast. And if *she* knew that, so did their killer.

Processing this and waiting for Mr. Bourn's emails, she called Palmer. It was early and there would be very little they could do right now, but she felt if they could somehow put the pieces all together and get in front of this, they could potentially have their killer by the end of the day—and hopefully before he was able to strike again.

CHAPTER TWENTY ONE

Camille was once again looking at the maps on the dry erase board when Palmer entered her office. It was 4:35 in the morning and it was already becoming clear that this was going to be an exceptionally long day. To his credit, though, Palmer seemed wide awake and in good spirits. When he plopped down on the loveseat, he looked at the dry erase board and frowned.

"We got tox results back in," he said. "So why are you back at the maps again?"

"Because Terry Winsome's file says she lived in the little town of Messer, which is about half an hour outside of the city. But more than that, there are two cities that each of the boats happened to pass by during their excursions. That could be another potential link. I'm also checking to see if any of the areas the boats traveled by would have been primary spots for cone snails."

"Yeah, I know you told me you thought the toxin likely came from some sort of snail, but I need more than that now that I'm awake. There are poisonous snails out in the water around here?"

"Yes. And typically, cone snails won't be able to kill you. Not if you're just stung by a single one. But the tox reports," she said, nodding to a few print-outs on her little coffee table, "indicate that the amounts of conotoxin found in the bodies—particularly in Brittany Gable—were more than just toxins from a single snail."

"So…what are you thinking?"

"I think we may need to consider the idea that someone is extracting the toxins from the snail. It sounds ridiculous on the face of it, but it's not unheard of. Even someone with the most basic of tools would be able to do it."

"Okay, but even if that's the case, the question is: *why* would someone want to do that?"

"I guess that's one of the several questions we need to answer," Camille said.

"You know, there's something else I think we need to look into as well," Palmer said. "But because it's so early, I think we might want to wait a bit."

“What’s that?

“Well, we know that Terry Winsome had done several of these tournaments in the past before her husband passed away. And each of the fishermen had sponsors. I’d imagine whoever sponsored Winsome had sponsored her before. I assume they’d know a pretty good amount about her and probably even the tournament itself. If Terry had some sort of super-secret spot she was hitting that’s out there in all those weeds and cutovers, her sponsor would probably know, right?”

Camille nodded, looking away from the maps for the first time in about ten minutes. “That’s a great thought.” She checked her watch and saw that it was 4:41. “But you’re right. It might be a little too early to start conducting interviews. In the meantime, I think we can maybe start looking through records and databases for deaths caused by conotoxins. It probably won’t take long because I doubt there’s been more than a dozen or so in the past few years.”

“You know, I hate to go there,” Palmer said, “but it sort of reminds me of that first case we worked together. The one where we ended up looking into that Haitian voodoo stuff. Wasn’t there a chemical down in Haiti that people were using to make people appear to be dead?”

“Yeah. Tetrodotoxin. It comes out of a certain kind of pufferfish.”

“So if voodoo priests down in Haiti can extract that sort of poison out of a fish without any fancy equipment, it stands to reason that your average Joe off the street could do it with cone snails, right?”

“That’s what I’m thinking. So we take that assumption and add it to the speculation that this guy knows the ins and outs of all of these sidewinding streams coming off of the Mississippi, and I think we’re dealing with a guy that likely lives somewhere relatively rural, but also a local that knows the city like the back of his hand.”

With a sigh, Palmer started setting his laptop up on the coffee table next to the tox screen reports. “Well then,” he said. “Looks like it’s time to go snail hunting.”

***

In the end, Camille’s estimate of a dozen deaths over the past ten years had been a bit too generous. There were two known deaths from the result of cone snails dating back as far as 1980. One of those had nearly come around and survived but upper respiratory complications from the recovery made things much harder, ultimately killing the victim.

It wasn't a very uplifting bit of research to lead them out of the office at 6:30, headed for Gil's Bait and Tackle—Terry Winsome's sponsor for her last five tournaments. Palmer had called Bob "Gil" Gilmore at six o' clock, only to find that he was already on the way to work, as he opened his shop up at seven o' clock during the spring and summer months.

When they arrived at the rather sizable bait and tackle shop, only one single fisherman was scanning the racks and aisles. The store was of a decent size, with lots of open space. It had the feel of a small, mom-and-pop place, almost like one of the smaller beach shops along the coast that seemed to be just barely hanging on.

They found Gil at the far right-side of the store, behind a long counter. Multiple styles of rods and reels hung on the wall behind him. Above all of the merchandise were mounted fish, everything from colorful trout to what appeared to be a small marlin. It all looked very professional and a good bit of fun as well. Gil looked to be in his early sixties, dressed in a tee shirt and khaki shorts. He had a well-maintained brown beard that hung down to his chest, and thick bifocals were perched on his nose.

"Agents," he said with a nod before either of them introduced themselves or showed their badges.

"Is it *that* obvious?" Palmer asked.

Gil smiled and said, "In here, yes. It's pretty obvious."

"Well, I wish we were visiting with better reasons," Palmer said. "I'm Agent Palmer and this is my partner, Agent Grace. As I told you on the phone, Terry Windsome was found killed last night, and we're sort if rushing about to get answers. We figured if you were her sponsor, you probably knew a good deal about her and how she approached these tournaments."

"Our concern," Camille added, "is that she may be one of several victims of what is looking to be a serial killer. So anything you can tell us could potentially save lives."

"Well, I know a good deal about Terry. I knew her husband first. Of course, he passed away not too long ago, and it destroyed Terry. This was the first tournament she'd participated in since his passing. She was excited to get back out there but I think there was some guilt, too. Fishing was always something she and her husband had done together."

"And what was the fishing community's opinion of them?" Camille asked.

"As far as I know, they were well-respected. There's not really much bad blood in the fishing circle around here. Just a bit of good-natured competition when these tournaments come around, you know?"

"Would you go so far as to say the two of you were friends?" Camille asked.

Gil thought about it for a moment and shrugged. "Not on a personal level. I sponsored her because she and her husband were always good customers. But I didn't really know much about her. I know she's got a sister that lives in the city somewhere. And I can tell you her favorite bait, her go-to lures, and things of that nature, but nothing too serious."

"Well, the fishing part of it may be more help than you think," Camille said. "Her body was discovered in a little aluminum boat, with her much nicer boat anchored a bit further down the river. We think that might mean she was navigating some of the off-the-beaten-path streams during that tournament."

"Wouldn't surprise me. She was always a bit of a risk taker when it came to landing fish."

"Would you happen to know of any secret spots she had?" Palmer asked. "Maybe places she kept secret because she was so successful there?"

"Oh, I'm sure she did. But in the tournament world, you're going to be hard pressed to find anyone that's willing to share that kind of secret with anyone other than very close friends."

"Not even her sponsor?" Camille asked.

"Nope, not even her sponsor." Gil looked legitimately sad that he wasn't able to offer anything else to the conversation. Then, slowly, a look of realization dawned on his face. "You know, now that I think of it, there was a bit of a fuss when Terry decided she was going to participate in the Caterwaul Tournament. She registered a few days after the cut-off date and they let her in anyway. I think everyone assumed it was because the people in charge knew about her situation, getting over her husband's death and all. Everyone seemed perfectly fine with it…except for one man. His name's John Bunker, and he just happened to end up winning the tournament yesterday."

"What kind of fuss are we talking about?" Camille asked.

"Oh, just raising hell about how it was unfair. And now, that's John Bunker's usual song and dance. Always afraid he's going to get slighted and isn't afraid to try to yell loud enough to get people on his side. It seems every year, he's griping about something: making sure everyone is properly licensed, trying to get people eliminated early because of so-called illegal bait. He' a real piece of work."

"Was there any face-to-face confrontation?" Palmer asked.

"No. Just a bunch of bitching on Facebook. People put him in his place pretty quickly this year, though. He shut up after a few days, when he realized this was a fight no one was going to join him in."

"Any idea where we might be able to find him today?" Camille asked.

"No clue. He's probably working. So if I were you, I'd check out the riverboat companies."

This caught Camille's interest at once. She felt a spark of hope, a thread starting to form that she thought might lead them to the end of this case quicker than she'd expected.

"Why would we contact the riverboat companies?" she asked.

"Oh, well, because John Bunker has a day job as a riverboat captain."

The revelation felt like a small bomb going off. Every now and then a lead was unexpected, but this one felt like a tiny earthquake.

"Do you know which company he works for?" Camille asked.

"Sorry, no."

"As a river boat captain, I'd assume he knows the rivers exceptionally well, right?"

"Oh, for sure. And he has no problem telling it to anyone that will listen. Now, I say all of this about him though I've never had any quarrel with him. But he's known to be arrogant and has this sort of...*snootiness* to him, you know? With him, it's more than just knowing the river because he's a riverboat captain. His family has been around here for at least three generations, and they've all been expert fishermen. If you go in just about any souvenir shop, his great grandfather is listed in those cheap paperbacks about local legends. So John rides that wave high. I have no doubt he *does* know the river well, but damn if people don't get sick of hearing about it."

That was all Camille needed to hear. After all, she'd become convinced that they were looking for someone with an intricate knowledge of the river. And now that they had a lead that also seemed to have a grudge against pretty much anyone that might not agree with him on any given topic, it felt like a substantial lead.

"Thanks so much for your help, Mr. Gilmore," Camille said.

They exited the shop, both with extra speed in their step. Though she'd gotten far too little sleep the night before, the excitement of a very strong lead had her feeling more motivated than she had since starting the case. And with the sun not even properly having gotten the day started, it was enough to make her truly believe they might have a killer in custody by the end of the day.

CHAPTER TWENTY TWO

He wondered how many more he'd have to kill before they got the message.

He killed two yesterday. Certainly that was enough to cause these river boat tours and special events like fishing tournaments to shut down. If he had to send the entire city into lockdown or a state of emergency, he'd consider himself victorious. There would very likely still be work to do afterwards, but then maybe he'd draw some attention to just how terrible the citizens of the city treated it.

He killed two yesterday. Maybe today he'd kill three.

It was certainly within the realm of possibility. He was getting a very early start today, sitting on a park bench at 6:30 in the morning, sipping from a coffee and looking over to one of the small docks in the area. A group of eight girls were standing there, waiting to get on a smaller riverboat called The New Orleans Queen. It was a stupid name for such a boat but it did match the cuteness of the small vessel.

He watched the eight girls, laughing despite the early hour. He guessed them all to be somewhere between sixteen and eighteen years of age. Five of them were wearing black windbreakers with MRHS SOFTBALL written along the back. It was nearing the end of summer, so he assumed this was some sort of little team-building excursion, being that the end of ball season was just around the corner.

Behind them, several others were waiting. One older couple kept looking to the fairly loud and energetic teen girls as if they were a nuisance. Smiling, he understood completely. Two of the girls in particular were leaning against the dock rail and talking incredibly loudly. One reached into her pocket and pulled out a hair tie to put her hair into a ponytail. In doing so, a bit of trash fell out of her pocket and into the river. She never noticed or, if she did, she did not seem to care.

He checked his watch. 6:38. The boat, he knew, didn't take off until 7:00. It was one of the first that would venture out onto the river.

He reached into the pocket of his own jacket and felt the tube. It was the same tube he'd used to pelt the dart into the neck of the woman at the fishing tournament—the same tube he'd used to get the poison into his first victim, a wide shot that had taken him right behind the ear.

He'd not had to use the darts on the other two victims; dashing a bit of the toxin into the young girl's drink and the older woman's coffee had been more than enough.

He knew he had to be careful. He'd nearly slipped up when he'd taken out the fishing woman last night. He'd damn near forgot to remove the little dart from her neck. Was he getting too cocky? Too confident? At the end of the day, he figured he'd eventually get caught. But that was a concern for much farther down the road. He figured he could easily take out another dozen or so before the inept authorities ever even had a clue where to start looking.

He did his best to remain calm. He sipped on his coffee and kept his eyes on the group of softball players, trying not to seem too obvious. He closed his eyes and tried filtering out the insipid voices of the girls, trying to focus on the natural and soothing sounds of the river. He found it and it calmed him a bit. It also served as a reminder of what he was trying to protect and just how precious it was.

It calmed him so much that by the time he got up from the bench and started making his way over to the dock, most of the anger rising up in him had faded. And when he stepped up onto the dock, he even managed to smile at the older couple that were waiting to get on the boat behind the group of girls.

CHAPTER TWENTY THREE

It was easy enough to find out some basic information on John Bunker, as he'd just won the Caterwaul Fishing Tournament the night before. Not only had he posted about the win on Facebook, but so had the riverboat company that employed him. It was a company called Mississippi Miles. There was a picture split into two photos: one was a shot of John Bunker from the previous night, posed with his winning catch of a thirty-nine pound catfish. The second was a picture of him in his captain's uniform aboard a riverboat. The title above the post read: **Come Congratulate Caterwaul Winner JOHN BUNKER as he resumes his place behind the wheel of the Mississippi Miles Riverboats!**

"This post says he's not expected to get back on a riverboat for another two days," Camille said. She was in the passenger seat, allowing Palmer to drive. She stared at the pictures and tried to figure out why the sight of the man's face unsettled her so badly.

She went back to his Facebook profile and read through his "About" details. It took only a few moments of reading before she stumbled across another bit of information that painted a large bullseye on John Bunker.

"Get this," she said. "Bunker is the co-owner of Mississippi Miles."

"Ah, so it's not that big of a deal that he just happens to be one of the captains."

"It seems like this is a smaller outfit…family-owned. I can't help but wonder if it's something that was passed down through his family." She tapped her phone a few times navigating to the Mississippi Miles webpage. After some scanning, she said: "They only have two boats, named *Mississippi Miles One* and *Mississippi Miles Two*. And it…"

She fell silent for a moment. Palmer looked over at her and smirked. "I bet you're coming to the same conclusion I'm coming to, huh?"

"The conclusion that any bad press from the other two companies could benefit a much smaller riverboat company in a number of ways?"

"Bingo," he said.

"The only thing that makes it all fall apart is the fact that Bunker would have been preparing for the tournament yesterday morning. I have no doubt he could have potentially run into Terry or maybe even followed her, and killed her last night. but the morning…that's a totally different thing."

"I suppose we could probably speak to the folks that organized the tournament," Palmer said. "Maybe find out when Bunker showed up."

Camille thought it all over while also continuing to look at his picture. Had she seen this man somewhere before? It certainly seemed so; she was getting a sort of itching sensation in her mind, the idea that she *should* be able to place him but couldn't quite make out why.

"Also," she said, still eyeing the man's face on her phone, "we'd be able to rule him out one way or the other simply based on his work schedule. For instance, if he was working on the night Brittany Gable was murdered, he's not our guy. And I feel certain that a job like *riverboat captain* means he keeps a pretty tight schedule. It also means there's going to be a big number of people that would have seen him."

"It's a good point. He feels like our guy but working as a riverboat captain and then getting ready for a fishing tournament really doesn't feel like it would leave him a lot of spare time to murder four people."

"True. But think about the timing yesterday," she said. "If he struck early enough with Natania, he might have been able to get started on the tournament at the right time. And with Terry Winsome, we *know* he was on the river at the same time. We can—"

Her words locked up in her throat when she finally understood why the sight of John Bunker's face was affecting her so badly. With building anticipation, she opened up her photos. She'd taken screen shots from the surveillance camera footage from the *Whistlin' Pig* when they'd been trying to find answers regarding the death of Kevin Pleasant. The photos she had were nothing more than pictures of the other people that had walked by the camera along the back entrance to the boat.

She flipped through her photos and came to a stop at the sixth one. "Holy shit," she said.

"Got something?" Palmer asked.

"He was on the *Whistlin' Pig* at the same time as Kevin Pleasant."

"You're kidding…"

"No, I'm not." She showed him her phone and, though he was driving, he looked over at the picture. She watched as the same look of surprise she'd just experienced came over his face.

He let out a whistle and nodded. "Yeah, I think we got our guy." He then pulled out his phone, placed a call, and set it to speaker mode.

He set the phone on the center console and it was answered on the fourth ring.

"Palmer, its entirely too early," a male voice on the other end said.

"Hey Ramirez. Good morning," he said, quite ironically. "You at the office yet?"

"No. Still at home. Leaving in about fifteen minutes because I don't report to work until most normal folks do."

"I enjoy our comical shenanigans, Ramirez, but I don't have the time right now, man. Look, do you still have remote access from home?"

"I do. Why?"

"I need to find out where someone is, and I need to know it right now. We're working a murder case and we need to nail this guy as soon as possible."

"What's the suspect's phone number?"

Camille quickly pulled up all of the opened tabs on her phone and selected the website for Mississippi Miles. There was the line directly to the company and then a cell phone. She hoped the cell would go directly to John Bunker but they, of course, had no way of knowing. She recited it anyway.

"Got it," Ramirez said. "You know how this works, Palmer. It might take about half an hour. I'll plug it in here, from home, and get back to you with the results."

"That's fine. Thanks, man. And just so you know, this case is at the tip-top of the bureau's list of priorities at the moment. Come through and I'll make sure your name gets dropped when we're being heaped with praise."

"Promises, promises."

Palmer ended the call and Camille simply looked at him. "Who was that?"

"Jasper Ramirez, a guy that works in the surveillance and records division. I partnered with him for a few months several years back, but his strengths are behind a keyboard and monitor, not out in the field. I give him shit about it all the time."

"And he'll get results?"

"Oh yeah. He said half an hour, but I guarantee you he'll get back to us within fifteen or twenty. He's really good." He shrugged and said, "So, what do we do in the meantime?"

"Just working on a hunch here," she said, "but let's head to the river."

"Sounds like a good hunch," Palmer said, making a U-turn to head back to the river and the docks along its edges.

CHAPTER TWENTY FOUR

Palmer's guess had been close.

It took exactly seventeen minutes for Ramirez to get back to them. Camille plugged the address in as Ramirez spoke it out loud, a bit amazed at the speed and fluency of it all. Sometimes she got so wrapped up in a case that she never stopped to truly appreciate the speed and efficiency the bureau was capable of these days. She knew, though, that part of the success they were having was because Palmer had called another agent that seemed perfectly fine with taking orders from people other than directors and supervisors. Palmer apparently knew the same sad facts she'd learned long ago: sometimes, agents got results much faster when requests for information were shared among agents rather than pushed higher up the food chain where red tape and supervisory roles often muddied up progress.

To make the situation seem even more aligned with their theories, the address Ramirez gave them was a docking platform just outside of the French Quarter. It was a platform used for fishing excursions and, not to Camille's surprise at all, smaller riverboats. When they parked in the small lot just to the side of the platform, they saw that people were already boarding the small, red riverboat that sat to the left side of the dock. It was a modest-sized boat that had a rather charming design; it looked almost like an old-fashioned tugboat at the front but the back was more open to allow for the stairway to the second level and an open floor space for passengers to move around.

"Christ, this guy doesn't stop, does he?" Palmer said. "Already staking someone out?" Camille could hear the excitement in his voice. She felt it, too, but tried to keep herself anchored before getting carried away. There was no certainty that their killer was on the boat, though her gut told her they were on the right path.

"For all we know, this could be one of *his* boats," she said. "So of course he'd be on board if he's the captain."

"Nope," Palmer said as they got out of the car. He pointed to the right side of the upper level's canopy. There, in distinct white script, was the name of the boat: *La Salle.* "You said his were both named Mississippi Miles, right?"

“I did,” she said, finally slowing herself to give into the promise and excitement of being on the heels of their killer. They could potentially have this thing closed and wrapped before rush hour traffic started clogging up the streets.

They approached the ticket kiosk at the entrance to the dock where only one other person was currently purchasing a ticket. Camille spotted a placard behind the cashier that gave the departure times for the day. They were approaching the boat on its first voyage of the morning, which took off from the dock at 7:55—just five minutes away.

They showed their badges and IDs to the woman who didn’t give them any trouble or ask any questions. Her eyes simply widened a bit as she gave a simple nod and allowed them to pass.

They hurried past the kiosk, walking along the dock with the Mississippi River sparkling in early morning sunlight all around them. As they neared the boat, Camille stepped in closer to Palmer and, without any warning, took his hand in hers.

“That’s awfully forward of you,” Palmer said, confused.

“I’m looking on the boat and don’t see all that many people,” Camille said. “I think anyone that might be watching their backs or keeping an eye out for trouble is going to notice two single people like us, dressed the way we are. But as a couple, it seems much less likely.”

“Agreed,” Palmer said. “But I’m not letting you get past second base.”

“You wish.”

“Am I a total dirtbag if I admit that yeah, maybe I do wish a little?”

They boarded the boat and as they slowly made their way along the back end, she wondered if it might have been a smarter play to have the woman at the kiosk alert the captain. It then made her think they might not be approaching this from the best angle. Why give the killer a chance to attack at all? They could split up, one of them staying at the back of the boat to keep Bunker from escaping while the other one hunted him down.

“I think we should find the captain,” she said softly, leaning into him. “Tell him to start the engine, play the charade like he’s going to pull off, but ask him to stall as long as he can. We need to get this bastard before the boat even heads out to open water.”

“You do that,” he said. “I’ll stay back here by the exit just in case he picks up the scent and makes a run for it.”

She liked that she and Palmer were on the same page. It wasn’t the first time he seemed to have read her mind during their short stint as partners, and it made her much more comfortable about chasing down a killer with him.

She let go of his hand and chose to ignore the little hiss of disappointment that Palmer let out. If there was anything she *would* change about him, it was his almost constant tendency towards jokes. She hurried along the right side of the boat, passing by a young couple and their baby, an older gentleman standing against the rails and slowly typing something into his phone, and several other passengers. She came to a small door along the boat's bow, marked with two words on a small, decorative sign. It read: *Captain's Quarters.*

She opened it and found a small set of stairs going up. As she stepped inside, she could already hear a male voice, speaking into either a phone or radio. "See any more cars pulling in?" He apparently got a negative reply because he sighed in defeat. "Forty-seven on board," he said. "Shit, it's barely even worth going out."

Camille started up the stairs, letting out a polite *"Hello?"*

There was the sound of movement and then a man of about fifty peered around a small half-wall and looked down the stairs.

"Ma'am, you can't be in here. This is—"

Camille showed her badge while saying, "I'm Agent Camille Grace, with the FBI. My partner and I are on board and are currently looking for a man suspected of killed four people."

"My God," the captain said as horror and disbelief spread across his face. "On my boat?"

"Yes, sir. For right now, I need you to do whatever you would normally do. I need you to do everything *except* pull away from the dock. Engine tests, announcements, whatever. But for now, please do not pull out into the river."

"Yeah, okay," he said, processing it all. "How long do you think?"

"You said yourself just now. There are only fifty or so people on this boat. So hopefully not very long. Now…are we good?"

"Yes, I understand."

"Thank you," Camille said, and headed back down the stairs. She came out of the captain's quarters and stepped back outside. As she did, a man passed by her, looking down to the deck. He walked quickly, as if he was trying his best not to be spotted by anyone, his head downcast even as he passed by Camille.

The behavior was suspicious enough to cause her to stop for a moment, giving the man a few more seconds of cushion before she started to follow him. She allowed two more passengers to funnel in between them and watched as he rounded the very front of the boat, heading to the rails at the very top of the bow.

When he stopped and pressed his back against the rail to turn and look back within the boat, Camille continued to walk. She did her best to observe him without being obvious, her eyes flitting about as those of any tourist would, trying to take in everything. She noticed that when her eyes did pass by the suspicious-looking man, he looked away and pretended to cast his gaze out to the water.

But he wasn't quite fast enough. Camille got a good, head-on look at his face. It was without a doubt the same man from the Facebook posts and the surveillance camera pictures. It was John Bunker. Slowly, Camille took her phone out of her pocket and texted Palmer. She did so with the skill of a decent actress, acting as if she were responding to a funny text or email, a fake smile spreading across her face. In the midst of her theatrics, she sent: **He's at the front of the boat. I'm going to advance but not interact just to see what he does. Be ready just in case he runs for it.**

She allowed the fake smile to fade from her face as she started walking to the front of the boat. She did not make a straight line to Bunker, but made it appear as if she were walking to the far right side, perhaps to lean over and get a better look at the river. As she did this, she felt and heard the engine start up. The captain was going about business as usual, just as she'd requested.

As if using this as a distraction of sorts, Bunker got to his feet and started walking away. When he did, he looked back just in time to see Camille redirecting herself and following after him. Camille knew what was coming next but was still a bit surprised when it actually happened.

Bunker started walking quickly, bumping against a woman drinking a cup of coffee and nearly causing her to drop it. When she wheeled around on him and said *"hey!"* Bunker escalated his rapid walk into a sprint.

Camille wasted no time. She gave chase, managing to avoid the woman that had nearly spilled her coffee. As she came around the corner, making her way down the aisle between the rails and left side of the boat, she could catch a clear view of Bunker about fifteen feet ahead. She was fortunate in that most of the passengers had opted to walk to the center of the boat, under a canopy where coffee and snacks were being served. The few that were walking along the little walkway saw her coming and stepped to the side with baffled looks on their faces. Realizing that her cover was blown, she figured announcing who she was might cause Bunker to stop.

"John Bunker," she shouted. "FBI! Stop running!"

Bunker did no such thing, though. He continued to run to the back of the boat. Camille followed closely behind, closing the distance between them. When she reached the stern, she got there just in time to see Palmer standing in front of the exit. He had his jacket pulled back a bit, revealing his Glock which he was currently reaching for as Bunker approached him.

"Stop right there, Mr. Bunker," Palmer said. "We're with the FBI and just need to ask you some qu—"

In a fast and unexpected movement, John Bunker dashed hard to the right. he took two steps and then did his best to jump over the rail. He nearly made it, but his left leg betrayed him at the last moment. It struck the rail with a hollow sound. Rather than jumping cleanly into the river, he spilled over, struck the side of the boat, and went into the river with an awkward splash.

As Camille rushed over to the rail, she heard Palmer say, "Well, damn."

Camille looked around for a flotation ring and though she did see two hanging along the rear of the boat, she saw something a little more promising behind them, anchored along the docks. There were two smaller boats, little pleasure craft vessels that she'd missed because she'd been so hyper-focused on the riverboat.

"Feel like driving another boat?" she asked Palmer.

"Maybe."

As they both exited the boat, leaping back out onto the dock, Camille saw that Bunker was desperate beyond reason. He was swimming away from the riverboat, heading in the opposite direction of the river—even though the opposite bank was at least one hundred feet away.

They reached the first of the smaller boats, the sort that was little more than a pontoon boat that held maybe twenty people at most. Naturally, when they reached the boat, there were no keys for the ignition. But before they could get too sidetracked and frustrated, there was a shout from the *La Salle*.

"Hey! Hold on!"

Camille looked back to the riverboat and saw the captain hurrying off of the boat, jangling a set of keys in his hand. For a moment, Camille thought he was going to toss the keys to them but he dashed across the dock and practically jumped into the little pleasure craft.

Palmer made a motion to reach for the keys, but the captain was already nestling himself behind the wheel, plunging the keys into the ignition. Without a word or even asking if he could assist, the captain started the boat. In a similar manner, Camille quickly started untying the rope from the dock.

"Get as close to him as you can!" Palmer called out over the engine.

The captain, who seemed very excited to be part of this, nodded. He pulled away from the dock and gradually increased the speed as he made his way around the side of the *La Salle.* By the time he'd cleared the riverboat, he'd gotten the smaller boat up to a good speed. Right away, they saw the floundering shape of John Bunker, already exhausted and only twenty or so feet away from the boat.

"What the hell were you thinking?" Palmer yelled as the captain pulled the boat up alongside him.

"I've done nothing wrong!" Bunker yelled, his breath labored and short as he tried swimming away from the boat.

Camille and Palmer pressed against the side as the captain steered so close that the side of the boat softly bumped Bunker. He let out a cry at the contact, a noise that was cut short by the agent reaching down, grabbing his shoulders and the collar of his jacket, and pulling him up on board.

Bunker hit the floor with a loud, wet thump. "I'm just looking out for the river!" he screamed. "I'm trying to protect the river!"

These were exclamations that, to Camille, pretty much slammed a few more nails in his coffin. He was admitting to their theory, that he'd been killing as a means of what he saw as protecting the river.

"That's admirable," Camille said, taking out her cuffs as Palmer pinned him down with a knee to the back. "And you can tell us all about your efforts to save the river from an interrogation room."

She cuffed him and when she got back to her feet, she realized that everyone aboard the *La Salle* was watching and, slowly, started to applaud.

All in all, it wasn't too bad of a way to start the day.

CHAPTER TWENTY FIVE

When they had John Bunker in an interrogation room at the field office, Camille didn't see much guilt in his expression or the way he was reacting to them. No, all she saw was anger. He resembled a kid that had gotten busted for bad behavior but seemed absolutely clueless what it was that he had done.

"You were up pretty early, considering you won a fishing tournament last night," Palmer said.

Bunker said nothing to this, though he did smirk a bit at the mention of winning the tournament. "I'm not saying a single word until I can speak to my lawyer."

"Fine," Camille said. "We'll arrange for that in just a second. Would you like us to wait until your clothes dry, though? I'm not sure how a lawyer is going to react to knowing that you fled before I even approached you and you were so desperate to get away from us that you tried—and failed—to jump off a boat and into the Mississippi River."

For the first time, Bunker's expression changed from anger to something resembling disappointment. Maybe, Camille thought, he was starting to understand what a mistake he'd made in causing such a scene out on the *La Salle.* Taking advantage of this little emotional hiccup, Camille started asking questions, choosing to ignore his request for his lawyer.

"We know that you're the co-owner of Mississippi Miles and that you're one of the captains of those ships. So it seems curious to us that you'd be on a competitor's boat. Want to fill is in on that?"

He looked as them as if he seriously couldn't understand why he was there. "Is…is that what this is about? Did you seriously arrest me for checking out the competition?"

Ooh, that's a good cover story, Camille thought. "Why don't you tell us what you were ding on the *La Salle* this morning, and then we'll tell you why we were looking for you."

"I just told you. I was checking out our competition. Mississippi Miles is a small operation, so I know we can't really hold a candle to the bigger ones. But lately, we've been struggling for business…sort of at the back of the pack. I've been scouting other small riverboats to see what we can change."

"And you thought that was a reason to run away from FBI agents?" Palmer asked.

He had nothing to say to this. In fact, Bunker pressed his lips tightly together, as if trying to ensure nothing damning would come out.

"Maybe if we tell you why we came for you, you'll be a little more willing to talk," Camille said. "It has come to our attention over the past four hours or so that you didn't care much for another of the participants in the Caterwaul Fishing Tournament. A woman by the name of Terry Winsome. Would you say that's correct?"

"Ah Jesus," he said. "Did she make some sort of complaint because I railed on her on Facebook? Is *that* what this is about? The FBI gets involved for—"

"She made no such complaint," Camille said. "And she won't be making those sorts of complaints in the future because she was found dead in a little rowboat last night, just before the end of the tournament."

"Dead?"

"Yes."

"Terry Winsome?"

"Yes. Do you need me to repeat all of that again?"

He shook his head, his eyes darting back and forth between Camille and Palmer.

"Mr. Bunker," Palmer said, "can you tell us where you were along the river between the hours of five and nine o'clock yesterday evening?"

"I mean…I can try. But it won't be exact…I was sort of all over the place after about three. I…" He stopped, trying to collect his thoughts. Or, Camille thought, trying to come up with a believable lie. "I spent the biggest part of the afternoon out on this little spot out near Bayou St. John."

"And did any other fishermen see you there?"

"Just two. They were…" His face turned to a mask of pure shock and this time when he looked at the agents, he looked absolutely terrified. "Hold on. Are you after me because you think I killed her?"

"Partly, yes," Camille said. "But I'm afraid it goes a bit deeper than that." She removed her phone and as she opened up her photos and pulled up the one she needed, she continued: "Five days ago, did you travel on a riverboat called the *Whistlin' Pig?*"

She could see that panic was starting to settle in as he did his best to recall. Slowly, he stared to nod. "Yes. In the afternoon. I don't recall the time."

"This is you, correct?" she asked, showing him the picture.

"Yes, that's me."

"Did you know that a passenger from that same expedition was found dead in the river the following day? He seems to have fallen overboard with slight signs of strangulation. There was also a small amount of a deadly and unique toxin in his bloodstream."

This time, he went as white as a ghost. He sat back rigidly in his chair and started shaking his head. "No. That…that wasn't me! I was on that boat for the same reason I was on the *La Salle* this morning!"

"Just comparing boats, right?" Palmer said.

"Yes! I've been doing it all around the city for the last two months or so! Comparing prices, the atmosphere, the attitudes of the staff, even the merchandise and little gift shops on some of them! I've been toying with the idea of opening up a third boat but wanted to have it offer the top-of-the-line features of other smaller boats in the area. And let's be honest…these bigger companies are destroying the river with their pollution and litter. Why shouldn't smaller, more environmentally sound companies be able to get a fair shot?"

Camille nodded and said, "During this two month period of time, have you ever been aboard a boat called *Wheeler's Delight?"*

"That sounds familiar, yes."

"Would you be at all surprised to find that a woman was killed and thrown overboard on that boat as well?"

His eyes started to water and for a moment, she thought he was going to get sick. "I didn't…I don't even know what you…no. No, I'm not saying anything else before I get a lawyer in here."

"Well, if you insist on that, we can do it," Palmer said. "But also know that we are currently eyeing you for the murder of four people, including Terry Winsome last night."

Camille had one more question, one she thought might help her to confirm Bunker was the killer even if he didn't say a word. "Mr. Bunker, how much do you know about cone snails?"

The look of confusion on his face was stark and seemed genuine. It seemed like she'd asked him a question in German and he was trying his best to translate it in his head.

"Cone…*what?"*

"Not important," she said dismissively. "Come on. We'll escort you to a phone so you can make that call."

And as she opened the door while Scott escorted him away from the table, Camille felt as if she was also opening the door for their killer, letting him go on in and do what he pleased. Because as far as Camille was concerned, Bunker simply wasn't their guy.

CHAPTER TWENTY SIX

Camille was drinking black coffee in her office as she and Palmer waited for John Bunker's lawyer to arrive. Palmer had just come back into her office, carrying his own coffee and a folder with what looked like ten or twelve printouts contained inside. Camille knew what conversation she wanted to have with Palmer and was already quite sure how it was going to go. It had only been twenty minutes or so, but she kept thinking back to the look of utter bewilderment on Bunker's face when she'd mentioned cone snails.

If she had to guess, she was pretty sure he'd had no idea what the hell she'd been talking about.

Palmer handed her the folder. "That's phone and credit card records over the past month for Terry Winsome. No clue if it's going to do any good, but seeing as how she's the most recent victim, digging as deep as possible might do some good."

She took the folder absently and wasted no time getting into the conversation. "You think Bunker is our guy?"

"I think all signs point that way. And if he wants to stay quiet while waiting on his lawyer, I'm perfectly content to remain convinced. We know he was on the *Whistlin' Pig* when Kevin Pleasant was killed. We know he had beef with Terry Winsome. He knows the rivers *and* the riverboat community very well. And then there was all of that bitching and screaming about wanting to protect the river." He sipped from his coffee, sighed, and then asked: "I take it you have doubts?"

"Did you see his face when I asked about cone snails?"

"I did. But it *was* a strange question. I don't blame the guy."

"It wouldn't seem so strange to someone that has been dealing with them recently. If anything, I'd expect a shocked or spooked face. A face that says *how the hell did you know that?* Also, we have no idea when he was on *Wheeler's Delight* or if he was ever on *Whistlin' Pig* a second time."

"Yeah, and we don't know those things because he's refusing to talk until his lawyer gets here."

"But you do understand that if we can't concretely confirm that he was on those boats when Natania and Brittany were killed, he becomes much less of a suspect."

"Yes, I know that."

"And if he did indeed see two other fishermen while he was fishing at Bayou St. John…"

"Yes, I know how this process works, Grace." He shook his head and smiled. "Sorry, that sounded pretty defensive. But for now, I sort of *have* to think this is our guy. You know what I mean?"

She did. They had four victims on their hands, two of which had been killed within less than twenty-four hours of one another. She wanted it to be Bunker, too. But her gut was telling her that his alibi and reasons for being on those other riverboats was legit.

"There's the anger, too," Palmer said. "When we pulled him out of the river, he was furious. I remember thinking: *yeah, this is the sort of anger that might push someone to strangle another human being.*"

"Another thing that puzzles me, though," Camille said, "is having three of the murders be on or around riverboats."

"Well, he knows them well," Palmer argued. "Seems like a fitting hunting ground."

"Yes, but if he's truly interested in quote-unquote protecting the rivers, how the hell is dumping bodies in it a sign of that? And on the flipside, as the owner of a riverboat company, murders on those boats wouldn't only hurt the business of the companies that owned the affected boats. You'd think it would be a blight on the entire riverboat industry."

She watched as Palmer considered this. He didn't argue it right away, but seemed to process it. In the silence, Camille started thumbing through the folder. The phone records showed that she didn't use her phone very often. Most of the calls were to the same number, another cell owner in the city. Camille recalled that Gil had told them that Terry had a sister; she supposed that's who she'd been calling.

The credit card reports told a similar story. It showed a snapshot of a woman that didn't get out much. There were listings for a local pizzeria, several Amazon purchases, two visits to Gil's Bait and Tackle, a few stops by grocery stores, three listings for gas, and a hotel stay. The hotel stay was the last thing listed and, because of that, Camille took immediate notice.

"Did you look through these?" Camille asked.

"No. They're literally hot off the press. Why?"

"Terry Winsome apparently stayed in a hotel the night before the tournament. I don't know if it's relevant, but it does seem a bit odd, right?"

"Maybe. I mean those tournaments start very early in the morning. Maybe she wanted to be in the city first thing upon waking. Her address is about half an hour outside of New Orleans."

She typed the name of the hotel into her laptop's browser. Three listings popped up. Two were located right in the center of New Orleans. The third was in the small town of Jensen Springs. It was a small town just ten minutes outside of the city proper—and roughly half the distance between New Orleans and the town of Messer, where Terry Winsome lived.

"Jensen Springs," Camille muttered, the name ringing an entire series of bells in her head. "Jensen Springs."

"It's a little nothing of a town," Palmer said. "What about it?"

Camille went back to her maps, still stuck up on the dry erase board. She easily spotted Jensen Springs just on the outskirts of New Orleans. It stood out, though, because it was one of the two cities that both the *Whistlin' Pig* and *Wheeler's Delight* passed through. At first, the connection seemed tenuous at best but then the full weight of what it could mean settled over them.

"The hotel she stayed in the night before she died is in Jansen Springs. The town is one of the two that both riverboats passed by. And being that we now know it was where Terry Winsome spent her last night alive, this small town is an official connection between all four victims."

He seemed a little doubtful, but Palmer still got to his feet and joined her at the maps. "But there's really nothing all that special about Jensen Springs. I think some tourists will stay there if they don't want the constant buzz and noise of New Orleans, but other than that…nothing. Unless maybe the killer lives there and is using it as some morbid point of reference."

Sorting it all out in her head, Camille used her phone to Google the phone number for Gil's Bait and Tackle. She called it and got an answer on the third ring. Gil's voice was instantly recognizable when he answered: "Gil's Bait and Tackle."

"Hello, Mr. Gilmore. This is Agent Grace, from this morning. I hate to bother you again, but I was hoping you could help fill in some more blanks for us about Mrs. Winsome."

"I'll certainly try. But like I said, I didn't know her all *that* well."

"Yes, I understand that. But in the dealings with becoming her sponsor and preparing for the tournament, did you have any idea that she stayed in a hotel the night before the tournament even though she only lives about half an hour away?"

"You know, I actually *did* know that. She made a point to tell me. Apparently, it was this little hotel in Jensen Springs that she and her husband had always stayed in the night before a tournament."

"Do you happen to recall if there was anyone else around when she told you this?"

"Oh, I can't recall. I know we were here in the shop when she mentioned it. So if there were other customers around, I guess anyone could have overheard it."

"Do you happen to know if there was anything especially appealing about this hotel to her and her husband?"

"Sorry, no. I just know the memories were the only real reason she decided to stay this time around."

Camille felt the potential thread unraveling and rolling away. "Thanks, Mr. Gilmore."

"Sure. Happy to help any way I can."

Camille ended the call. She then sat down behind her laptop and, with the browser still open, searched for *Jensen Springs riverboats.* She scrolled past the ad listings and clicked on the first actual list.

"I'll be damned," she said as the started reading.

Palmer came up behind her and chuckled. "See. I'm telling you, Bunker is our guy."

Fourth of the list of eight riverboats that routinely passed through or even took off from Jensen Springs was a joint entry for *Mississippi Miles One* and *Mississippi Miles Two*. The star ratings that visitors had left behind showed that maybe Bunker had reason to start snooping on his competitors after all.

But the second listing was a boat called *Stukey's Sweetheart.* Based on what she read, it was a reconstructed steamboat that was growing in popularity among locals and tourists alike because of its unique design. Furthermore, on the schedule that was listed by it, she saw that *Stukey's Sweetheart* had left from a dock in New Orleans and would be docking in Jansen Springs for more passengers. And it was set to arrive in forty minutes.

"Right there," Camille said. "I'm getting on that boat."

"Grace…why can't you just rest happily with the guy we've got in an interrogation room with quite a few arrows pointing at him?"

"Because *all* the arrows aren't pointing at him yet." She stood up and slipped on her jacket. "But it's a just-in-case visit. You're welcome to stay here with Bunker, just in case his lawyer gets here soon and he feels like talking."

"Okay, so why *that* boat?"

"The killer is stepping up his game, killing more frequently…like he feels the need to do it is urgent. It's growing in popularity, which means more passengers. And our guys seems to have some obsession with trying to keep the river…what? Safe? Clean? I don't know. But also, the timing on this one would be to his advantage and it's yet another one with that Jensen Springs connection."

"So I stay here and hang out with the potential killer while you go for another ride on the Mississippi?"

"Yeah, seems like it."

He considered it for a few seconds but shook his head. "You go, and I'll stay here. But when you get back and find that Bunker has confessed, don't come crying to me."

"We'll see," she said with a nervous smile as she headed for the door.

***

Camille knew she was racing the clock, even as she sped out of the parking lot. Getting on board would not be a problem; even if they were sold out of tickets (which was unlikely given this time of year *and* the time of day) she'd easily work her way on by showing her badge to the right people. But even beyond that, she thought there might be a much simpler solution. It was a very long shot and she figured she may very well piss a few people off, but she had to try.

As she blasted through a red light, honking her horn, she set her cell phone to speaker mode and called McCutcheon. The call was answered on the second ring, a clear indicator of just how much the case meant to the bureau—because it meant so much to the city and its commerce.

"Agent Grace, how are you?"

"I'm fine, but I have a favor to ask and it's going to seem a little extreme. I think I may have a lead on the killer and to keep from causing a scene, I'd like to request that all riverboats be stopped for the space of about two hours."

There was a heavy silence on the other end of the line. It was a silence she'd sensed before, the kind that was typically followed by a bit of chastising.

"Agent Grace, there's no way we could do that. By the time it was all coordinated and accomplished, your two-hour window will have come and gone. Besides that, it would be a big, neon indicator to the public that something is going on. Not to mention you and I would both be answering a ton of questions from the city government in the coming days."

"Okay," she said, not surprised but still a bit disappointed. "What about just one particular boat? There's one that's headed for a dock in Jensen Springs that I strongly believe could end up being—"

"Forgive me for interrupting, Agent Grace, but I'm confused as to why you're gunning for boats anyway. The last update I received stated that you and Agent Palmer currently had a suspect in custody—a man named John Bunker. That's correct?"

"Yes, ma'am, but I'm following up on loose ends."

"Oh, I see. Well, while I certainly appreciate the thoroughness, it is not nearly enough for me to strike fear into a river boat captain, company, or its passengers. So follow up on whatever leads or loose ends you have, but no…I can't demand a riverboat shut down due to nothing more than speculation."

Camille wanted to argue her point further, but the irritation in McCutcheon's voice was unmistakable. Hearing it, Camille understood. If she were to shut down operations of *Stukey's Sweetheart* and Camille's hunch turned out to be wrong, there would be an immense amount of backlash for both of them.

But as she neared the dock, Camille started to feel that this was more than a hunch. She was suddenly certain that Jensen Springs was integral to the case. And while she was not prepared to say Palmer was wrong on his certainty about Bunker, she did think he might be resting a little too peacefully on just a few connections rather than a solidified answer.

She raced in the direction of Jensen Springs, hoping that she was wrong. because even though she did feel as if she was dead on the money with their killer using the town as a milepost of some sort, she had no such certainty that he might wait to strike.

Hell, for all she knew, their fifth victim could be dead and bobbing in the water right now.

CHAPTER TWENTY SEVEN

Because it was still relatively early in the morning—her dashboard clock read 9:13—Camille was blessed with relatively thin traffic. She made the typical half-an-hour drive in under twenty and arrived at the dock seven minutes before the boat was set to take off. As she hurried away from her car and onto the dock, she saw that *Stukey's Sweetheart* was already at the end of the dock, letting passengers on and off. It sputtered a slight cloud of exhaust into the air, its engine growling in a delightful and somehow peaceful way.

Camille knew that this was just one of many stops. There was a small chance the killer, if he was eyeing this boat at all, wasn't even on board yet. Or, on the other hand, maybe he'd been on since it shipped out in New Orleans and he'd already selected his next victim.

With just enough time to spare, Camille opted to go a bit undercover this time. She approached the small ticket kiosk along the space between the parking lot and the dock, acting like any other paying customer. As she was handed her ticket, she noticed a small rack of snacks pushed all the way to the left-side of the kiosk counter. It was fairly basic: candy bars, mints, gum, and lollipops.

An idea quickly came to her and, acting solely on a whim, she said: "Can I get a pack of gum, please? Spearmint."

The lady behind the kiosk handed over the gum, taking a dollar in exchange. Camille pocketed it and made her way onto the boat. She started to feel a bit silly, maybe even a little over-reactive, as she stepped aboard. What if she went through all of this trouble while Palmer was back at the station with the *real* killer—a killer they'd already caught and stopped. She wondered if there was something inside of her that simply couldn't accept such an easy victory. After all, Bunker *had* clumsily fallen into the river when trying to quickly make an exit from a riverboat. Then again, maybe that was another point in her favor. A man that had been secretly killing people for a week was probably a bit smarter than that. As she sorted through all of this, she began to slowly make her way around the boat. She kept an ear out for anyone that sounded aghast or terrified of anything that had happened during the trek from New Orleans to Jensen Springs.

Apparently, it had been an uneventful trip. Of course, no one had known the other riverboat victims had died until much later—long after both boats had returned to their docks of origin. As she walked around to gauge the moods of the passengers, she also got a good look at the ship. She could understand why it was considered a popular up-and-comer. It had a sort of antique charm in the steamboat feel, but there were touches here and there that made it feel very sleek and modern. This included a small bar and patio area on the second deck that felt more like an actual lounge than a riverboat.

She found an open seat in the lounge area and allowed herself to once again go over the key details of the case. She was starting to wonder if the inclusion of poison might be more important than she thought. If the killer was strangling his victims, why bother with the toxins? Why go through the trouble of not only acquiring such a tool but then being crafty enough to administer it? She supposed it could be sort of a back-up…if the killer perhaps failed in killing his victims, maybe the poison was used to simply make sure the deed was done one way or the other.

But why would someone bent on killing even think of carrying out murders if they thought they might be incapable of it?

She started to wonder if the killer might have a disability or was simply weak. If either of these was true, there would certainly be a need for the conotoxin. She recalled that the coroner reports had all showed signs of strangulation but no immediate damage to the throat or larynx—indicating that the killer may not be very strong at all. Maybe the killer needed some other means to help overpower his victims. And if they could somehow find this out for sure, it would make the hunt for the killer a bit easier. It would also eliminate John Bunker from contention.

The sound of laughter broke her attention. She got up from her seat and walked over to the rail. Looking down from the lounge area, she saw three young children standing with an adult by the back of the boat. They were feeding pieces of bread to several ducks that were swimming happily back and forth. One of the kids, a girl that appeared to be no older than five, found it particularly amusing.

Watching them throw the bits of bread overboard made her heart sink a bit. Would this killer be so low and despicable as to murder children? If trying to protect the river and the environment was indeed this guy's MO, these three kids could very well be angering him—if, of course, he was on the boat at all.

She smiled down at the kids and returned to her seat. She brought out her phone and went back to the screen shots she'd saved from the *Whistlin' Pig*'s security footage. As she scanned through the twenty-two images, she kept her eyes out for men of small stature, either short or just frail-looking. The only person fitting the description was an older gentleman that was walking with a woman of the same age, likely an old, retired couple out for some time on the river. The man was very tall but remarkably thin.

The only other small-statured or petite males she saw were kids. There was a boy that looked to be twelve or thirteen, a teenager of sixteen or so, and one boy walking with his parents. He was walking with his head cast to the side, looking away from the camera. Squinting her eyes at this, Camille used her fingers to enlarge the picture, zooming in on the boy. At a closer glance, she saw that the boy wasn't *actually* walking with the people she'd thought to be his parents. He had angled himself between them and was walking slightly behind them. When she really studied the picture, it looked as if the two adults had no clue the boy was behind them.

And he's looking away from the camera, she thought. *It's like he knew it was there. It's like he's been on the boat before and knew when to look away.*

Camille zoomed in a bit closer, stopping when the image became too grainy. She could only see the slightest bit of the right side of his face, just the cheek and the slightest bit of hair. She supposed it *could* be an exceptionally small man. Also, weren't most teenage boys tall beasts that hit their growth spurts between twelve and fourteen or so?

With that realization in mind, she became fairly certain that the figure she was looking at was an exceptionally small man—no taller than five foot three. At that height, wouldn't he likely need some sort of assistance to render his victims incapacitated?

With a growing bit of speculation in her gut, Camille took a screenshot of her enlarged picture, zoomed in, and sent it to Palmer. She followed it with a text that read: **Thinking the killer might be an uncommonly short male. Think of the weak strangulation attempts and the need for assistance RE: conotoxins. Think of how easy it would be to pass as a child on a riverboat if you're of short stature.**

With that sent, Camille once again got out of her seat. She glanced around the lounge area and saw no one that fit the description. There was a group of women enjoying mimosas at the small bar as they waited for the boat to hit the river again, and a twenty-something couple taking selfies over by the rail opposite Camille. She looked past a man in a suit, reading something on his phone, and a Korean couple speaking animatedly with the bartender. A bit outside of the lounge area were six girls wearing identical windbreakers. Along the back in a bold, white font was: MRHS SOFTBALL.

Feeling slightly on edge now, Camille made her way back down to the first floor. After all, she assumed it would be easier for a killer to toss the body into the river from the lower deck. When she was downstairs, she spotted a small figure right away, sitting alone on a bench near the front of the boat. He was hunched over, peering intently into his phone.

She walked slowly but with purpose over to him. As she got closer and was about to engage him, she saw an older man standing not too far away, speaking to someone else. The man peered back to the small figure, as if checking on him. Camille walked by, glanced in his direction, and saw that it was clearly a teenaged boy. He appeared so small because of the way he was sitting, hunched over his phone.

She then remembered the kids with the ducks. She hurried in that direction, to the stern. She could no longer hear the laughing, but she saw that the ducks were still floating about, searching for more easy snacks. As she drew closer to the back, she saw one lone figure, dressed in a basic denim jacket. She could tell from the side that it was a male, and he was peering into the water, in the direction of where the kids had been tossing their bread.

There were no parents nearby and though it was hard to tell from the way he was leaning against the rail and looking away, she was quite sure it was an adult male. Camille took three hurried steps towards him, ready for anything. She felt the cuffs at her back, the Glock holstered to her side, all hidden by her jacket. She passed by six people, weaving her way through a few others that had just stepped on board.

Behind them, a crew member closed the entryway gate and the boat started to move away from the dock. The engine was terribly loud for a few seconds and then lowered into a gentle hum. As the boat began to move through the water, Camille continued forward.

She approached the man quietly, stopping directly behind him. "Are you waiting for someone?" Camille asked

The figure turned quickly, spooked by her sudden voice. Right away, Camille was filled with embarrassment. It was a man that had to be at least eighty. There was a little glimmer of excitement in his eyes from having been spooked and a growing smile on his face at the sight of the young, pretty woman that had approached him.

"Waiting for someone?" he asked with a raspy laugh. "I suppose so. Aren't we all?"

Camille smiled back, red-faced and wondering if she was maybe pushing this a bit too hard. "I suppose we are," she said. And without any further explanation, she added: "I'm so sorry to have bothered you."

The old man watched in confusion as Camille walked away. She felt awful, having disturbed the old man's peaceful morning on the river. He seemed to have taken it in stride, though.

Now that the boat was on the move, she knew she had to act fast. She had one more trick and she knew it was an act of desperation. She reached into her front pants pocket and took out the pack of spearmint gum she'd purchased at the kiosk. She then walked to the front of the boat and positioned herself where anyone that happened to look in that direction would see her. With a bit of dramatic flair, she tore open the pack. She tossed the plastic wrapping off the boat and into the river.

She was surprised just how guilty it made her feel. She then plucked a piece of gum out of the package, unwrapped it, and popped it into her mouth. The wrapper followed the plastic packaging, going right into the river. She then unwrapped the other four sticks of gum in the package and, one by one, tossed the wrappers overboard. She noticed that a few people were giving her nasty looks but no one was quite brave enough or concerned enough to say anything to her.

Camille then stepped away from the front and started walking over to the side, back towards the stern. She tossed the sticks of gum into the water as well, tossing them out far enough so that anyone looking out to the water would easily see them.

With her little plan carried out, she felt slightly ridiculous. What if her hunch was wrong? What if all she'd accomplished was attracting a few dirty looks from the passengers and littering up the river?

The sound of a scream from overhead shoved her doubts aside for a moment. The scream was so loud and so sudden that it had her reaching for her Glock right away. She did not draw it, but kept her right hand hovering there as she looked up to the second deck. There was another scream, the sound of commotion, and then a female cry of despair.

With her hand now falling to the Glock and ready to draw it at any moment, Camille raced for the stairs leading to the second deck.

CHAPTER TWENTY EIGHT

Camille had no problem spotting the source of the screams and commotion when she got to the second level. Off to the side of the lounge area, the girls wearing matching softball windbreakers were in a state of panic. One of them was being held up by two others, while the remaining members of the group were moving around with no clear goal in mind. Camille did see one of them over by the bar, speaking urgently with the bartender. The dozen or so people sitting in the lounge area and bar were looking over with irritated interest and disgust.

As Camille made her way over to the girls, she saw the vomit on the floor. She also saw a few spilled drinks with little chunks of ice and deep colors—slushies or smoothies, she supposed. The moment she spotted this mess, the girl that was being held up by her friends added more to the pile. One of her friends was so grossed out by it that she released the girl's arm, nearly causing her to stumble and fall.

Camille dashed forward, taking a wide breadth of the vomit, and took the now-freed arm. "You okay, there?" Camille asked.

"Uh-uh," the sick girl said.

Camille looked to the other girl holding the sick girl up, a tall blonde, and asked: "What happened?"

"No idea. We were drinking these slushies and joking around, and then Kelly just started puking. It sort of happened out of nowhere! She was fine one moment and then she—"

Kelly started to retch again but this time nothing came up. It was little more than a dry heave. Still, Camille could tell from the way the girl was sagging that she had no power in her. She was on the verge of fainting or simply collapsing from the exhaustion of whatever was wrong with her.

Camille thought of Brittany Gable, puking into the river before being choked and tossed overboard. And with that comparison, a thought came into her head like a bullet: *He's here. The killer is here, on this boat, and this girl, Kelly, is supposed to be his next victim.*

Camille's eyes searched the group of girls, looking for the one that seemed the calmest of the group in the face of this unexpected disturbance. She saw a short brunette that had come back from the bar with a small bucket filled with soapy water and rags.

"You," Camille said, nodding to her. "Listen to me. I'm with the FBI and need to quickly search the boat. I need you to take over for me here, okay?"

The brunette nodded and quickly came over. She took Camille's place under Kelly's left arm, her eyes now wide and alert at the mention of an FBI agent in their midst.

"All of you, listen to me," she said, scanning the group of girls. "At any point in the past fifteen minutes or so, did Kelly step away from the group?"

"Yeah," the tall blonde said. "She went to the bathroom a while ago."

Camille looked at the spilled slushies on the floor of the second deck, worried. "Did she take her drink with her?"

"I...I don't know," the blonde said.

"I'm pretty sure she did," another of the girls said.

Camille looked around and saw that two chairs behind them were open. She dashed over to them and pushed then together. "The two of you need to get her off her feet. I think she may have been poisoned." She looked at another of the girl and said: "You…go to the bar and get her some water."

She looked back to the smallish brunette that had taken her place at Kelly's left arm. "Has anyone unfamiliar come up to your group during your time on the boat?"

"A few, yeah."

"And where did you guys get on?"

"Back in the city. At the dock off Port Barley."

"Were any of these people men on the shorter side?" Camille asked.

"Yes!" one of the other girls said. "He was sort of irritating at first but then…just creepy. And Kelly was sort of joking about running into him again when she came out of the bathroom."

"Any idea where he might have gone?" Camille asked.

"Well, he was actually up here like five minutes ago. Kept looking over here at us. I thought he was just checking us out, you know, like a pervert."

Or keeping tabs on Kelly to see how she was doing, Camille thought.

"Did he leave before Kelly started throwing up?" Camille asked.

"Yeah," one of the other girls said, pointing to the stairs. "Like maybe a minute before. He looked really pissed about something—like he was looking down to the water and got super mad for some reason. He sort of stormed off down the stairs."

My gum wrappers and gum, Camille thought. *Damn. I must have just missed him.*

She nearly started for the stairs but then another thought occurred to her first. "Is this all of you? Are you missing anyone?"

"Kiara," the tall blonde said. And as she went on, genuine concern came over her face. "She…she went to the bathroom like a minute or two before you came up. She said her stomach was feeling weird."

Camille turned and ran for the stairs, fearing that there was no time left for questions—that she may, in fact, have already wasted too much time.

Her intention in dropping the trash and gum into the river had been to lure the killer into coming after her. But in the end, it had served as a distraction of sorts. She had no idea if the killer had been going after Kelly or this new girl, Kiara, but Camille thought her plan may have bought both girls a bit of time.

She raced down the stairs, slowly drawing her Glock. She passed by two people, very lightly saying: "Step aside, FBI," so they could hear it but no one else could.

She'd seen the restrooms during her initial sweep on *Stukey's Sweetheart*, so she knew they were downstairs, situating along a little corridor that connected the port and starboard sides of the boat. She had to nudge her way through a few people milling about, probably curious to see what all the commotion up on the second level was about.

She came to the corridor and nearly collided with an overweight man coming out of the area. She was short, but not as short as the man she was looking for. The man saw the gun in her hand and backpedaled quickly away.

"Step aide," she hissed. "FBI."

He pushed himself against the wall and inched away as Camille passed by. She came to the little concave-style room that gave way on the right and left to the restrooms—the men's on the right and the women's on the left. She rushed into the ladies room, instantly thrusting the Glock out in front of her. It was a small restroom, offering only three stalls and a small sink. Only one of the stalls was occupied; she could see a pair of simple flats and bare ankles in the space between the bottom of the stall door and the floor.

"Kiara? Kiara…with the softball team? Is that you?"

"No," a woman's voice snapped back. "I'm not Kiara. And I'd appreciate some privacy!"

Had the bastard already struck? Had he nabbed Kiara before she even made it to the restrooms?

Camille turned around and exited, heading directly into the men's room. Maybe, she thought, he'd nabbed her and carried her into the men's room to attempt strangling her. But when she got to the men's room, she found only one empty stall and three empty urinals.

"What the hell?" she muttered.

She rushed out of the men's room and back out into the corridor. In doing so, she once again nearly collided with someone. It was a man in a crewman's outfit, the same outfit worn by all of the boat's staff.

"Ma'am," he said. "Someone wanted me to make sure you're indeed with the FBI." He looked at the Glock nervously, his voice trembling with worry.

"Yes, yes," she said, aggravated. She used her left hand to pull out her badge and ID. "I'm trying to remain discreet," she said. "I believe there may be a killer on the boat, actively trying to kill someone right now. I need you and however many others you can find to keep watch along the rails to make sure no one tries to push or throw someone overboard. Also…are these the only restrooms?"

"N…no," he said, now very nervous. "We have one other near the captain's quarters. If there are emergencies or something like a mother needing to change a diaper, we'll allow passengers to use them."

"What about if someone gets sick?"

"Yes, ma'am. That, too."

"Where?"

The crewman pointed behind him, to the starboard side. "Take a right. It's the first door you'll come to, and then, once you're in that room, it's the door against the back wall."

Camille hurried off in that direction. She didn't like that word was spreading along the boat that there was an FBI agent on board. If that news got to the killer, there was not telling how he might react. In other words, she had one more reason to hurry.

She came to the door along the starboard side the crewman had mentioned, already aware that there were people watching from the back end of the boat. She opened the door, Glock once again held out in front of her, and made her way into the small room beyond. There was a door to her left, leading up to the captain's quarters, and then, just as the crewman had said, a door all the way to the back. She ran to it, grabbed the knob, and turned.

It was locked.

Had she been a little clearer-headed and not feeling as if she was racing against the clock, Camille may have thought a bit more rationally. But as it was, she was filled with dread and urgency. She took a step back, leveled her gun to the knob, and blasted it off with two shots. Splinters of wood rained down and the knob hung loosely down. She raised her leg, kicking the door in and partially stumbling inside.

In the space of the second that she allowed herself to regain her balance and take in the scene, her heart was flooded with fear and anger in equal amounts.

A small man was on his knees, one pinned to the chest of the young woman beneath him. His hands were around her throat and the woman was barely able to fight against him. Her eyes were dazed and glassy, looking up to the ceiling in an almost disinterested gaze.

The man looked at Camille and released his grip around the girl's neck at once. But rather than raise them into the air, he reached into his pocket and took out a needle…a small one that almost looked like a strange dart. But then, as more was revealed, she saw that it was more of a very small syringe. As he moved, there was a fraction of a second where Camille nearly pulled her trigger. But he was simply too close to the girl, hunkered down over her. The slightest error and she could hit the girl—presumable Kiara—as well.

"Back away," the man said as he pressed the needle into the girl's throat. "She's only knocked out right now. But what's in this will kill her."

"Put it down," Camille said.

But he seemed to understand that he had the upper hand here. He lay down flat against the girl, the fight now completely out of her. He knew Camille wouldn't shoot while he was in such tight proximity.

"We can work this out," Camille said.

"I'm not stupid. If you found me here, you know what I've been up to. You know what I've been doing. Now you step away or I'm going to kill her. I'll stab her right in the neck, and if the puncture to her throat doesn't do it, what I've got loaded into this needle sure as hell will."

Slowly, Camille took a step back. She had no intention of obeying him but did know that even a few steps away would make him feel confident—that it might cause him to slip up a bit. All she needed was an inch or two of space before she'd get a clean shot.

But as she took her second step back, the man made a very sudden movement. It was so fast that Camille worried he'd decided to stab Kiara in the throat, anyway. But no, that wasn't right. He was bringing that odd syringe up to his face. In doing so, Camille saw that it was more of a tube. And by the time he got it to his lips and blew hard on it, she finally knew what it was.

But it was too late by that point. A sharp and searing pain exploded along the left side of her chest. She looked down and saw something thin and silver protruding from just above her breast.

She fumbled for it, still a bit in shock over what had happened. She found it with her free hand and grabbed it, but even as she pulled it out and dropped it to the floor, she knew the damage had already been done.

She could feel the warmth spreading along her chest as the poison started to circulate. She stumbled and looked back to the man, already wrapping his hands around Kiara's throat again.

Knowing she only had precious seconds before she'd be just as incapacitated as Kiara, Camille charged forward. But the world was already tilting and going fuzzy around the edges, her knees like jelly, as she stumbled back towards the restroom in one last effort to save this girl's life and put an end to the killer's plans.

CHAPTER TWENTY NINE

Camille had a very brief moment to understand that the killer wasn't used to his victims putting up a fight. This became clear when he froze up as she came charging forward. When he finally started moving again, he freed one of his hands from around Kiara's neck and reached back into his pocket, probably for another of those little darts. But he'd wasted too much time.

Camille attempted to propel herself at him, almost like a football tackle. But when she put all of the weight into her knees to do so, she found that her balance was far too compromised. She felt herself falling down instead. So, with her last bit of sense and energy, she made sure to carry all of her weight forward. This allowed her to fall inside the restroom rather than in a useless pile to the floor.

She fell directly on the killer who was, in turn, lying on top of Kiara. In a tangled pile of limbs, Camille did her best to orient herself. But she could feel whatever he'd injected her with—a conotoxin if her hunch was correct—spreading quickly. She felt like she was drunk and having a panic attack all at the same time. Deep down in her stomach, she could feel a churning sensation. And wouldn't that be something? To puke while in a tangled pile of bodies.

As she tried pushing herself away from the killer, he managed to plant an elbow directly in her chin. It rocked her head back hard and she could feel her teeth clink together. Ironically, the jolt seemed to clear her head, even if only for a fleeting moment. In that moment, she understood that she was still partially on top of him and that the Glock was still in her hand. She tried leaning to the right but was stopped by the wall. And from there, any which way she turned herself, she could not get a clear shot that would not also run the risk of hurting Kiara. Instead, she gripped the Glock tightly and slammed her hand down hard on the side of the killer's face. She felt something crunch under her fist and then she was pushed hard to the left. She hit the floor and almost right away, she felt a clamping sensation on her right wrist.

The killer slammer her hand into the floor and then started digging his fingernails into her skin. It burned right away, and she could feel blood drawn. But it was all happening in another world—or so it seemed. The moment of clarity went spinning out of control and she once again felt nothing but the spreading heat of the poison and the sensation that the boat was sinking. Only, it was not sinking into the water, but some strange tar-like substance. Her stomach buckled and her lungs suddenly felt as if there was no air left to draw in.

She tried to scramble to her feet but one of her legs was still caught in the tangle that was her, the killer, and Kiara. She tried pulling at it but it did no good. She was just too weak. The fuzzy edges of her vision were slowly growing dark and in a blinding moment of fear, she also realized that the killer had managed to knock the gun out of her hand.

She could just barely see him as he reached for it, his hand falling around the butt. He was bleeding from the nose and there was madness in his eyes. But beyond his leering face, the world was a blur of colors that were growing darker and darker.

The killer raised the gun and then the shot came.

Camille felt nothing. But the world grew even darker.

And somewhere in that darkness, the killer was screaming.

Camille felt blood rushing over her chest and the side of her face. *I'm dead,* she thought. *A few more seconds...and I wasn't able to save her...I wasn't able...*

She felt a stirring of air above her, the killer moving quickly away from her. And with it, he continued to scream. Through his screams (*wait, is that a scream of pain?),* she heard something else, too—something that made no sense. Someone was calling her name. A man, his voice urgent and fearful.

"Camille! Camille, you have to hang in there with me, okay?"

She tried very hard to focus, trying to pry the darkness away and see through it. Was that...?

"Palmer..."

God, it was so hard to breathe. And what the hell was Palmer doing here? Maybe she *was* dead. Maybe she was dead and her last logical thought before slipping away was of Palmer.

But then she felt his hands on her shoulder. She was being sat up and something slipped over her face. For a moment, she could breathe. It felt like being born again, and the darkness evaporated for a moment. Her entire body still felt like jelly, as if she hadn't slept in days and had just now finally allowed herself to collapse into bed.

Palmer was there. Beyond his shoulder, she saw several fuzzy shapes occupying the small room beyond the employee's restroom and the captain's quarters. Three or four people, moving frantically around. One of them was laying on the ground with another man pinned on top of him.

"Palmer? Shot…he shot me…where…and the girl…"

"Quiet, Camille. Just—"

"Step aside, Agent Palmer," came another voice. "We need to get a better look."

She felt Palmer move away and then two other people were there—a man and a woman positioned on either side of her.

"Agent Grace, do you know where you are?" the woman asked.

"On a boat. *Stukey's Sweetheart.*"

"Okay, good. We know you're having some trouble breathing, but just hang on, okay?"

"Yeah."

She heard more commotion around her as her vision started to fade again. "Agent Grace, I'm going to give you an injection, okay? In your chest, so it might—"

But Camille didn't hear the rest of this. Instead, her mind seemed to cave in, leaving behind a monotone image of a large back yard, a pig pen, and rolling storm clouds hanging in the air.

"It's okay," Camille said to the woman at her side. "Daddy said to leave the pigs alone, not to go in there with them. He was keeping…keeping me safe."

And with that, the image was wiped away, leaving Camille to the darkness.

CHAPTER THIRTY

It turned out she hadn't been shot. She learned this from Palmer roughly five hours after she'd been removed from *Stukey's Sweetheart* and was lying in a hospital bed. He'd brought in a can of ginger ale and was pouring it into a cup for her. After handing it to her, he settled down in the bedside chair and looked at her with something close to admiration.

"Well, I figured that," she said. "When I came to and saw no bandages, I put two and two together. But…the doctors said they wanted you to be the one to tell me how it all went down."

"First," he said, "they're telling me you can leave after they do one more battery of tests. Turns out you were right about a lot of things concerning this case, chief among them being the use of conotoxins. They gave you some meds that knocked it right out. The doctor I spoke to said you had a nasty dose of it, but he doubts it would have been fatal."

"What about the girls? Kelly…Kiara?"

"Kelly is fine. Sort of in the same boat you're in. Kiara, though, is going to be in the hospital for few days. She suffered a broken collar bone from the skirmish in the bathroom and the amount of conotoxins in her was a bit extreme."

"So…the shot I heard…?"

"That was me. Got the bastard high up in the shoulder. Tore though some artery and blood just went everywhere. You, uh, well…you got a lot of it on you."

"How were you even there?" she asked.

"Because the moment I got your text, I left the office and came out. Made some calls to make sure I could get an assist. The moment we pulled up alongside the riverboat on the game warden's speed boat, we heard the nervous murmurs of the people on board. And then one of the crew members told us there was something going down near the captain's quarters' restroom." He paused here and let out a shaky sigh. "If I'd been a single minute later, that girl might be dead. And you…well, I don't know. And I don't want to think about it."

"Is the killer going to make us jump through hoops? Does he have *any* sort of story or attempt to try weaseling out of this?"

"Don't know. I haven't spoken directly to him just yet. But the State Police are searching his house and I've already been informed that he has a very rustic set-up in his basement that would be more than capable of extracting toxins from cone snails."

Camille sipped from the ginger ale, thinking about what else she might have missed while blacked out. "So what else was I right about?"

"About Bunker not being the perfect fit. And I'm sorry as hell I was so stubborn on that. With McCutcheon so adamant that this thing get solved ASAP, I was just eager to wrap it. I sort of got blinded by that and…I'm sorry." He reached out and took her hand. "If I'd gone with you, you probably wouldn't be in a hospital bed right now. How are you feeling anyway?"

She kept her hand in his, surprised at how comforting it felt. "Just very tired. Sort of have a headache." She took a while to pay attention to her body a bit more and added: "And my stomach is sort of cramping."

"The docs said you may experience some nausea and headaches as your body kicks the toxins out."

"How long are they saying I'll be in here, anyway?"

"If the next batch of tests come back clean, they're saying you can be discharged after that. I think they plan to run those tests this evening and have the results pretty quickly."

Camille nodded. She also realized that the area where she'd been hit with the killer's dart was rather sore. As she and Palmer sat in silence, he slowly and almost resentfully removed his hand from hers. "Get some rest," he said.

"Good idea."

"Do you…do you want me to stay?" There was a look in his eyes that made her think he wanted her to answer in the affirmative.

"Your call. But I really don't want you watching me sleep. So…no. Go to the office and be present at the tail end of all of this. I'm sure McCutcheon will be around and one of us should be there."

He nodded and walked to the door. He looked back before he opened it and when he set his eyes on her, Camille wasn't sure she'd ever seen him so serious and concerned before.

"This scared the hell out of me" he said. "I know we've only been working together for a few months now, but I've grown to trust you more than anyone else I've ever worked with. Hell, more than just about anyone I know. I just need to be better at following your lead. I should have come with you. I should have—"

"Stop it. I was the one that suggested we split up."

"Yeah, but if I was smarter, I would have argued it and insisted I come with you."

She smiled. "It's cute that you think you could sway me like that. *Insisting.* Give me a break."

He smiled but there was something more in his eyes. Warmth? Compassion? She didn't know. But what she did know was that it caused her heart to skip a beat and made her want him to come back to her bedside and take her hand again.

"See you in while," he said. "Great work today."

"You, too."

Palmer left the room with his head down, closing the door slowly behind him. Camille looked at the door with an uncertain glance, wondering why she felt as if she missed him already.

***

The following day as Camille made her way to AD McCutcheon's office, her phone buzzed in her pocket. She was fully expecting it to be Palmer, as they hadn't spoken since he'd left her hospital room the day before. And she was quite certain that the strange little spark she'd felt between them wasn't only in her head.

The text waiting for her wasn't from Palmer, though. Quite the opposite; it was from Zack Hayes. **I'm officially in town. I think we should do dinner tonight. Seems a smarter move than the first official date being the memorial service for a woman you've never met.**

The message had her chuckling in the elevator on the way up to the second floor. As she responded back, she was amazed at just how good she felt. She supposed it had something to do with the fact that between her stay in the hospital and her deep, undisturbed sleep back at her apartment after getting home at eleven last night, it was the best she'd slept since arriving in New Orleans.

Sounds good, she replied**. Just let me know where and when.**

The elevator door dinged and she stepped out into the hallway. The last communication she'd had with McCutcheon had been a brief text exchange just before she'd been discharged from the hospital. In it, McCutcheon had told her she could have the entire day off if she wanted it, but she had requested a single meeting between the two at eleven in the morning. The late hour of the meeting was how Camille had managed to get in such a refreshing span of sleep and it also made her think the meeting would be of the light-hearted and congratulatory sort. Oddly enough, Camille had never done well with that sort of meeting. She preferred meetings that resulted in constructive feedback and maybe even a bit of pressure. They simply felt a bit more motivating.

She found the door to McCutcheon's office open. Her director was sitting not at her own desk, but a small conference table that sat off to the rear of the office. She had several thin piles of print outs stacked up on either side of a laptop. She looked up from her work when Camille entered, giving a cursory knock on the doorframe.

"Ah, Agent Grace. Thanks for coming in this morning. It really does mean a lot, given what you went through yesterday. But the doctors told me you came out of it like a pro, is that right?"

"I suppose so. I feel pretty great today, truth be told."

"Good. And if you'll have a seat, I think I may be able to make you feel a bit better." She waited for Camille to take a seat before she went on. "I expressed to both you and Agent Palmer that this case was considered urgent and of high importance. Given what you had to work with and what you were up against, I feel that you did an exceptional job. And I'm not the only one. I got a call several minutes before I texted you last night—a call straight from the mayor. Everyone is very much pleased with how things turned out. Now, there's some grumbling coming from a few self-important folks on the city council because of the scene that went down on *Stukey's Sweetheart* yesterday, but I'm choosing to tune all of that out.

"If you want my take, I'm *glad* you caused a scene. In a day and age where cops aren't trusted by the public and no one cares much for the government, it's nice to have a reminder of the sort of work we're capable of. I like to hear people talking about the efforts and successes of my agents. And you gave everyone something to talk about yesterday."

"Thank you," Camille said. She feared she was getting red in the face, as she'd never handled words of praise and affirmation particularly well.

"I do need to ask you a few other things," she said. "Particularly about Agent Palmer. I've spoken to him and got his story as to why he wasn't on the boat with you. Was it a mutual decision for you two to go your different ways yesterday?"

"Yes ma'am. And given that we *knew* there were so many people looking for this case to be closed, we thought it was the smartest play—to send one of us out on a hunch that our killer may still be out there while a strong suspect was in custody. Two birds, one stone."

"Yes, I figured as much. A good decision as far as I'm concerned. Now, speaking of Agent Palmer…do you feel the two of you work well together? The results of this case seem to indicate that you do, and he also believes so. He has nothing but praise for you. But how about you? What would you say if I suggested the two of you become long-standing partners. Any case you get, he comes along and vice versa. I'd start to view you as a team rather than looking to assign cases individually."

The thought was surprisingly exciting. She'd already started to think of Palmer as a partner, despite the lack of official titles. "I'd actually prefer that," she said. "We work well together. In the short time we've known one another, we seem to have somehow formed a sort of link. The same hunches here and there, and we fill in the gaps the other may leave behind."

McCutcheon smiled and leaned back in her chair. "Agent Grace, that's exactly what I wanted to hear. And between you and me…I think this whole situation is going to do you some favors in the bureau and the city. We might even be able to get you out of the basement office."

"Can we skip that?" Camille asked. "I rather like my little space downstairs."

"Then that's where we'll leave you," McCutcheon said. "Now, take the rest of the day off. Take tomorrow, if you want. Just make sure to touch base with me again in two days' time."

"Yes ma'am. Is that all?"

"It is indeed. Damned fine work yesterday, Agent Grace."

Camille took her leave, exiting McCutcheon's office with a huge win under her belt and an excellent partner officially assigned to her. Smiling, she thought about calling Palmer to let him know. but when she took her phone out, she was reminded of the text she'd received from Zack Hayes just before the meeting.

Well-rested and with heaps of praise from her director, adding on her first real date in over four years was going to make for an unforgettable day. She could only hope it was an indication of what this new future in New Orleans might look like for the long haul.

CHAPTER THIRTY ONE

Camille had nearly forgotten what it was like to live through the final hour or two before a date. There was pleasant anticipation and a desire to be prompt, but not over-eager. But after getting dressed in a simple pastel blouse and her best pair of jeans, she realized that what she *really* needed was a drink. And because she was already dressed and far too anxious about the night to come, she went ahead and arrived the restaurant Zack had chosen half an hour early.

It was a slightly upscale place, making her wish she'd dressed a bit better. But when she garnered the appreciative gaze of two men upon walking from the hostess area into the bar, she figured she'd done perfectly fine. It was a slightly upscale twist on most restaurants in the French Quarter, though this one was a bit outside what was traditionally seen as the Quarter. The bar was classy and dark, the restaurant floor carried the look and feel of a strange but appealing mix of farmhouse and colonial, and the entire back wall consisted of a stage. Currently, a three-piece outfit was playing a low-key sort of jazz, consisting of just drums, a stand-up bass, and a scrawny black-haired woman with a sultry voice.

She found a free stool at the bar, ordered a martini, and turned towards the stage. The band was currently playing a refined and surprisingly great version of a Bjork song—not something you expected from jazz musicians in New Orleans. As she sipped from her martini, the band started to remind her of Nanette.

Nanette had also been a big proponent of taking unexpected songs and flipping them on their head in either a subtle jazz rendition or even zydeco styles from time to time. Camille couldn't help but smile as she recalled a period of about two weeks when Nanette had worked with her band to figure out a way to make a Nirvana song fit the style. The result had been an amazing version of "Polly" that became a staple in their shows later on.

Later on, Camille thought. Following that period of Nanette's life, there hadn't really been much *later.* She was gone less than six months following those moments.

She shook those thoughts away, instead turning her attention to the date. Being in the bar, drink in hand and listening to the music, had helped a bit. But even as she prepared for Zack's arrival, Palmer wasn't too far from her mind. Yes, there had been…well, *something* between them when he'd been in her room at the hospital. But that could have easily just been him being rocked by the realization that they'd had a close call—that she could have potentially died. That was a feeling that would terrify anyone, even if there was only a platonic relationship between them.

She wasn't sure why she was so hung up on it, anyway. She didn't see Palmer in that way, after all. Did she?

Maybe this isn't the best thing to be thinking about while waiting for Zack, she thought. So she sipped from her drink as the band casually entered into an old Leonard Cohen song that she recognized but didn't know the name of.

And again, as if by some strange musical magic, her thoughts were snagged right back to Nanette. One of her groups had done a Cohen song. "Famous Blue Raincoat" maybe. Camille wasn't sure.

Despite the way the day had gone, with her amazing stretch of sleep, the praise from McCutcheon, and now this date, Camille found herself growing incredibly sad. It tended to happen whenever Nanette came to mind. There were just too many questions, too many things unresolved and—

With a flush of emotion coursing through her, Camille downed the rest of her drink. She slid the martini glass to the edge of the bar, flagged the bartender down, and pointed to it to let him know she wanted another. She then got up from her stool and found the little hallway to her right that led to the restrooms.

She pulled her phone out, standing against the rear wall. Without even thinking about it, she pulled up Deanna's number. She did have a bit of hesitation when she elected to make a FaceTime call. Something about it seemed almost too personal and, no pun intended, in-your-face.

But she pressed the button anyway. The phone rang three times before it was answered. When Deanna's face came onto the screen, her face stared back with a confused expression; it was pretty clear that Deanna didn't routinely take FaceTime calls. The phone was jostled for a few moments before Deanna seemed to make sense of what was going on.

"Camille?"

"Yeah, D. It's me. I want to know everything about Nanette. I want to know what was in the letter she sent you from Juarez. I want to know why she came to *you* of all people twelve years ago after she'd disappeared."

She saw the hurt and unexpected shock in Deanna's eyes. And God forgive her, she enjoyed it. She supposed it's why she'd chosen to make the FaceTime call. She wanted to see Deanna's reactions.

"I told you, Camille. I *will* tell you. But not over the phone. The last time we spoke, I told you we could have dinner and I would tell—"

"When then? When do you want to have this dinner?"

"Whenever you want."

Camille fought every urge within her to recommend they have it tomorrow. Everything within her *wanted* to recommend it but she knew she needed time to cool down. "A week from now. Next Monday."

"That's fine. My house, six o' clock." Deanna sounded uneasy, maybe even a little nervous. "Camille, are you okay?"

"Yeah. I'm starting to piece my life together and this…this stuff with Nanette is the final bit of it. Her, Dad…I need to know all of it."

"Okay. But…can you not tell your father?"

"Why not?"

Deanna shrugged. "Because I may just tell you some things he'd prefer to keep a secret. And I don't…Jesus, Camille. All of this is a mess."

Camille caught motion right at the top of her field of vision. The front door to the restaurant opened and Zack stepped in. He was eyeing the place as he pulled out his cellphone.

"Next Monday," Camille said. "I'll see you then. For now, though, I have to go."

She did not say goodbye or offer any other such nicety. She simply killed the call and pocketed her phone.

As she walked back towards the bar, her phone buzzed. She didn't bother checking it. She could see Zack lowering his phone, having just sent her a text. As she stepped into the bar, she waved at him. With a smile, he came walking over. He was dressed in a very basic polo shirt and khakis. He was a bit taller than she remembered but just as handsome.

Camille sat at the stool where the bartender had replenished her martini. Zack took the stool beside her, eyeing her drink. "And here I was, thinking I was going to look lame by getting here fifteen minutes early."

"Not lame at all," Camille said. "As far as I'm concerned, you're right on time."

Zack ordered a beer and asked to have their names be put on the wait list for a table. When he had his beer in hand, he looked longingly at her. "Yeah, you're as pretty as I remembered."

"That's good, I guess."

"Hey, let me ask you something. I was looking at the news in my hotel today and saw this thing about the FBI busting up some maniac that was killing people on riverboats. Did you have anything to do with that?"

She was laughing out loud before she even knew it and it was hard to make herself stop.

"Did I say something wrong?" Zack asked, uncertain.

"Not at all. It's just been a crazy few days."

He smiled at her in a way that made her feel the same way she'd felt when Palmer had left her hospital room. Without taking his eyes away from hers, he said: "So tell me about them."

"You sure?"

Zack nodded, and she told him. And slowly, the sound of the band faded into the distance and with it, thoughts of her past and how they had been holding her down.

With Zack beside her and the good news of the morning's meeting with McCutcheon, there was no place for the past. Not for now, anyway. Now, it was easier to look into the future; and over the rim of a martini glass and in the eyes of the man sitting beside her, it looked pretty damned good.

But even then, as she peered at Zack over the rim of her drink, her mind was already drifting to Deanna and the secret she might have to reveal.

NOW AVAILABLE!

<u>NOT HER</u>
(A Camille Grace FBI Suspense Thriller—Book 4)

Tourists are disappearing on airboats deep in the Bayou, and in this new novel by #1 bestselling and critically-acclaimed mystery and suspense author Kate Bold, Camille Grace, a rising star in the FBI's BAU unit, must face a diabolical killer and face the one place she vowed she would never return: the deep South.

"Phenomenal debut with a huge creep factor… So many twists and turns, you'll have no idea who the next victim will be. If you love a thriller that will keep you awake well into the night, this book is for you."
—Reader review for *Let Me Go*

A riveting psychological crime thriller full of mystery and suspense, the CAMILLE GRACE mystery series will make you fall in love with a brilliant new female protagonist. Packed with twists and turns, her story will keep you flipping pages late into the night.

Book #5 in the series—NOT NORMAL—is also available.

"This is an excellent book… When you start reading, be sure you don't have to wake up early!"
—Reader review for The Killing Game

"I really enjoyed this book… It draws you in right away and keeps you turning the pages right up to the end. I am really anticipating the next book."
—Reader review for Let Me Go

"WOW what a great read! Talk about a diabolical killer! Really enjoyed this book. Looking forward to reading others by this author as well."

—Reader review for The Killing Game

"Excellent start to a new series… Get this book and read it, you will love it!"
—Reader review for Let Me Go

"Captivating and riveting serial murder with a twist of the macabre… Very well done."
—Reader review for The Killing Game

"Good read with good plot, plenty of action, and great character development. A thriller that will keep you awake into the night."
—Reader review for Let Me Go

Kate Bold

Bestselling author Kate Bold is author of the ALEXA CHASE SUSPENSE THRILLER series, comprising six books (and counting); the ASHLEY HOPE SUSPENSE THRILLER series, comprising six books (and counting); the CAMILLE GRACE FBI SUSPENSE THRILLER series, comprising five books (and counting); and the HARLEY COLE FBI SUSPENSE THRILLER series, comprising three books (and counting).

An avid reader and lifelong fan of the mystery and thriller genres, Kate loves to hear from you, so please feel free to visit www.kateboldauthor.com to learn more and stay in touch.

BOOKS BY KATE BOLD

ALEXA CHASE SUSPENSE THRILLER
THE KILLING GAME (Book #1)
THE KILLING TIDE (Book #2)
THE KILLING HOUR (Book #3)
THE KILLING POINT (Book #4)
THE KILLING FOG (Book #5)
THE KILLING PLACE (Book #6)

ASHLEY HOPE SUSPENSE THRILLER
LET ME GO (Book #1)
LET ME OUT (Book #2)
LET ME LIVE (Book #3)
LET ME BREATHE (Book #4)
LET ME FORGET (Book #5)
LET ME ESCAPE (Book #6)

CAMILLE GRACE FBI SUSPENSE THRILLER
NOT ME (Book #1)
NOT NOW (Book #2)
NOT WELL (Book #3)
NOT HER (Book #4)
NOT NORMAL (Book #5)

HARLEY COLE FBI SUSPENSE THRILLER
NOWHERE SAFE (Book #1)
NOWHERE LEFT (Book #2)
NOWHERE TO RUN (Book #3)

www.ingramcontent.com/pod-product-compliance
Lightning Source LLC
Chambersburg PA
CBHW030613310726
48979CB00003B/694